P9-BYQ-779

Everywhere Blue

JOANNE ROSSMASSLER FRITZ

HOLIDAY HOUSE NEW YORK

Copyright © 2021 by Joanne Rossmassler Fritz

All Rights Reserved

HOLIDAY HOUSE is registered in the U.S. Patent and Trademark Office.

Printed and bound in April 2021 at Maple Press, York, PA, USA.

www.holidayhouse.com

First Edition

1 3 5 7 9 10 8 6 4 2

Library of Congress Cataloging-in-Publication Data

Names: Rossmassler Fritz, Joanne, author.

Title: Everywhere blue / by Joanne Rossmassler Fritz.

Description: New York : Holiday House, [2021] | Audience: Ages 8–12.
  Audience: Grades 4–6. | Summary: Twelve-year-old Maddie, who suffers
  from anxiety, loves music, math, and everything in its place, but when
  her older brother Strum disappears from his college campus, her family
  starts slipping away from her.

Identifiers: LCCN 2020035850 | ISBN 9780823448623 (hardcover)

Subjects: CYAC: Novels in verse. | Missing persons—Fiction. | Brothers and
  sisters—Fiction. | Anxiety disorders—Fiction. | Family life—Fiction.

Classification: LCC PZ7.5.R73 Ev 2021 | DDC [Fic]—dc23

LC record available at https://lccn.loc.gov/2020035850

ISBN: 978-0-8234-4862-3 (hardcover)

For my mother,
and in memory of my father

Part One

DIMINUENDO

November

November pulls me down.
Like a *diminuendo* in music,
gradually dying away.
Darkness falls too early
and the chill creeps in.

Before dusk,

> before we learn the truth
> about my brother,

this day plays out
like any ordinary day,
a symphony of sameness.

Just the way I like it.

At 2:46 in the afternoon
I duck out the main doors
of Margaret Murie Middle School,
frowning as I avoid
the straggly line of kids
waiting for buses.
Glad I'm not in that line today.
Emma waves. "Bye, Maddie!"
I wave back with a grin.

Fridays mean oboe lessons.
Gripping my instrument case
and hunching my shoulders
against the cold,
I walk four blocks west
to my music teacher's house.

I love walking.
If I lived in the city,
instead of boring old Bennett Corners,
I'd walk everywhere. Especially
the Kimmel Center, for concerts.
But I'm only twelve.
It'll be years before I can move
to Philadelphia.

As I walk up Mr. Rimondi's driveway,
I count my steps.
Eleven. An odd number
is not a good number.
Something will go wrong.

I could add an extra step,
      a tiny one,
but that would be cheating.
Dread fills my chest like cold sludge.
This will not be a good lesson.

Crushed leaves
rotting against the stoop
smell like the turkey feather
I use to clean the saliva

from my oboe,
especially when too much spit
clots the feathery tips together
into a sodden lump.
The leaves smell of mold and sadness
and leftover rain.

They smell of
November.

My Real Name

"You're late," Mr. Rimondi says.

But he smiles his crooked smile
so I know he's only kidding.
I glance at the big clock on the wall
above the music stand,
with the red second hand
sweeping past the two,
and smile back.
If I can make him laugh,
maybe
it will still be a good lesson.

"Twelve seconds. Not *that* late."

He throws his head back and laughs,
a bright, brassy sound like trumpets.
"Madrigal, you could be a metronome.

You're so precise." He wipes his eyes
with a handkerchief, chuckles some more.

Mr. Rimondi is the only one who uses
my real name.
Everyone else calls me Maddie,
except Aria calls me Mad
and Strum calls me M.
They both hate the musical names
our parents gave us.

But I like them.
They define us as a family,
even if sometimes
there is dissonance.

My Oboe

While my reed soaks
in a small cup of warm water,
I assemble my oboe,
gently screwing in each piece
in the right order.

Order is good.
Order is calming.
Just like even numbers.
Order helps me to
stop thinking bad thoughts.
About me throwing up.

People bleeding.
Or someone dying.

The last thing to be inserted is my reed.
It tastes earthy,
the way fallen leaves smell
before they get wet.
Oboe reeds are fragile.
Twin pieces of cane carved out
and pressed together.

My best friend, Emma, plays the clarinet,
which uses a wider single reed,
sturdier and less breakable.
Clarinets also sound different—
deeper and mellower.

Oboes sound a lot like ducks.
That was why Prokofiev
chose the oboe to represent a duck
in *Peter and the Wolf.*

Peter and the Wolf

There is an oboe solo
in *Peter and the Wolf*
that's so beautiful
it makes my throat burn.

That solo reminds me of the time
Daddy took us

to see *Peter and the Wolf*,
performed by the Philadelphia Orchestra,
when I was seven.

We sat in the second tier,
the three of us bookended
by Maman and Daddy.
We were all riveted.

Well, Strum and I, anyway.

Aria was eleven.
She yawned a big fake yawn,
pretending to be bored.
Probably hoping Strum would
agree with her.

When the oboist played the duck's theme,
I tugged Strum's arm. "Listen," I whispered.
"Isn't it beautiful?"

Strum was fourteen then.
He didn't talk to me much.
But that evening,
Strum leaned over,
blue eyes wide open.
"You're right.
It makes my body
hum. And it feels like...
like coming home."

I'm only the second oboe
but I want to play that solo
in the school orchestra's
winter concert,
which is three months away.
I'll need to work hard
to prove I'm good enough.

Perfect

Today's lesson is "Morning Mood"
from *Peer Gynt Suites*
by Edvard Grieg.
I love this song. It's bright and uplifting.

I begin to play,
my chest filling up with the notes,
swelling from the magic.

I concentrate on my embouchure,
the proper shaping of my mouth
to achieve the perfect vibration.
The perfect sound.

Everything must be
perfect.

Not Good Enough

Afternoon sunlight filters
through the dusty window and
falls across my sheet music.

The notes wobble
as I get distracted.

Sunlight makes me want
to be outside.
Exploring the woods or
swinging on our old swing set
in the sunny rectangle
of our backyard,
while Gizmo finds interesting things
to sniff under the shrubbery.
Gizmo is really Strum's dog,
even if he sleeps in my room now.

By the time my mother arrives
to pick me up
it will be dusk. Almost dinnertime.

Too late.

I'm allowed to walk from school
to Mr. Rimondi's house.
But I'm not allowed to walk home.
"It's too far," Maman always says.
"Et trop sombre." *Too dark*.

The squeal when I miss the G-sharp
makes me wince and hunch my shoulders.
How could I do that?
My fingers slow down as I keep playing.
The tempo lags.

"Again," Mr. Rimondi says.
"You're hesitating too much
in this piece.
It should be a lilting, pastoral tune.
You're making it a dirge."

I'll never be good enough.

My hands start trembling
so I count the measures.
Onetwothreefourfivesix.
Even number. Good.
It puts me in my safe space.

Deep breath.

I'm calm again.

Mr. Rimondi taps his pencil
on the sheet music. *Taptaptap.*
"Focus, Madrigal. Try it again."

I blow too hard. *Kraark!*

"No, no," he says, still calm,
still patient.
He points to his stomach.

"Breathe in from here.
Then breathe out slowly."

I know this.

And I know the notes
but I can't find the *feel*
of the music,
can't figure out how to create emotions
that simmer and fizz and boil inside
until they need to burst out
as melodies,
      as beauty,
           as magic.

When I hear recorded music,
I recognize the *feel,*
especially when my father
plays a vinyl record.

But I can't produce it myself.
And that's frustrating.
Could I really be a metronome?
Something mechanical
and not human?

The Importance of Punctuality

Finally, it's four-thirty and I can escape.
I jam the turkey feather
into my oboe to clean it.

Not a good lesson.

My stomach wobbles.
I take apart my oboe
and fit each section into its
proper place in the crushed velvet
of my instrument case.
This should calm me but
it doesn't.
I say goodbye and thank you
to Mr. Rimondi.
He smiles. "See you next week."

I walk outside
and peer through the darkening gloom.
Stand in the empty driveway,
dazed, wondering why
my mother's car isn't here.
Tap my foot over and over.
It's unusual for Maman
to be late.
She's a teacher.
A voice coach.
She knows
the importance of punctuality.

Something Is Wrong

Something is wrong.
Seven cars whizz past on Maple Lane

and I can't stand still. I'm jumpy
and tingling.
Finally, the gray Toyota
swings into the driveway.
Headlights sweep
over me and illuminate
Mr. Rimondi's garage door.
Flaking paint mars the lowest board.

I glance into the car, shocked
to see not my mother
but Aria.

I yank open the door.
"Where's Maman? Why are *you* here?
I thought you couldn't drive
after dark yet.
That's the rule."

I try to steady my voice as I
duck into the passenger seat but
my hands are shaking and it takes three tries
to hook my seat belt.
Something is wrong.

The Moment Everything Changes

Aria shakes her head.
"Mad, calm down."

Her eyes are red.
Her skin pale.
Has Aria
been crying?
My heart tumbles.
Down and down.
What is wrong?

She starts to back into the road
but a car honks as it roars past,
startling us both.
"Sorry," she says,
pianissimo, like a whisper.

I swallow hard.
"That's okay. I shouldn't
have distracted you."

She pulls more smoothly
into the road,
turns right at the light,
and heads south for home.
"Maman's a mess," she says.
"Dad's with her.
The police called."

My pulse pounds. *Whoosh whoosh.*
The police?
"Why?" My voice sounds small
in the wide darkness of the car.

She clears her throat.
"It's about Strum."
Strum? Strum's in trouble?
"What did he do?" I ask.
"Get drunk at one of those college parties?"

Aria's hands grip the steering wheel
so hard her knuckles turn yellow.
"No."
She inhales sharply.
"Strum disappeared."

The World Swirls and Falls Away

Wait.
Maybe I didn't hear her right.
"Did you say...
he *disappeared*?
You mean like, he's *gone*?"
Aria nods.
My heartbeat speeds up and my
breath catches. I picture my lungs
collapsing, unable to suck in air.

The world swirls
and falls away,
like one of those carnival rides
Strum took me on last summer.
The room spun around
faster and faster

until the floor dropped out
from under us. *Whoosh.*

Aria turns the car into our street
and pulls into our driveway
behind Daddy's SUV.
She stops the car
but we don't get out.

She rubs her eyes.
"Mad, just listen to me.
No one knows anything for sure.
Strum walked away from campus
yesterday afternoon.
But he didn't take his phone
or laptop. He left
most of his things
behind."

Why wouldn't Strum take
his phone?
My pulse thunders in my ears,
whoosh WHOOSH
whoosh WHOOSH.

Time Comes Unstuck

Aria tosses her long dark hair
over her shoulder.

"The police were called in
because Strum's roommate
reported him missing today.
He never came back
last night.
He didn't show up
for classes
today."

She takes a deep breath.
"And Maman is freaking out.
So we need to help her. Okay?"

I nod,
even though I'm confused.
Maman is the strongest person I know.
"They'll find him, right?
He'll be okay, won't he?"

"Of course."
But Aria won't look me in the eyes.

Strum, where are you?
Inside my head
French horns growl
like the wolf in *Peter and the Wolf.*
Everything seems unreal.

An hour ago I was thinking
about the crushed-leaf taste
of my reed
and mid-November darkness.

Thinking about
how hard I'll need to work
so I can earn a solo.

Now, all that seems
as if it happened a long time ago.
Time has come unstuck
and I don't know if I've been
in the car for weeks or days or hours
or only a few seconds.

Running

Aria opens her door. Climbs out.

No.
I can't.
Can't go in the house.
I want everything still
in its place.
Strum back in college
and everything right with the world.

I won't think about what
Aria said.

Closing my mind to her words,
I shove open the door
and run.
Legs pumping,

shoes smacking the cracked flagstone path
around the side of the house and into our
small backyard.
Leap onto the swing,
where I know I'll be safe.

Then Gizmo runs out, barking.
Gizmo.
Strum's dog.

Woof! Woof! Woof!
I jump off and
cover my ears.

Cement Wall

My mind hardens,
a cement wall between me
and the world.

Strum *can't* be missing.
He's at college
in Colorado,
studying wildlife biology.

If I call his phone
he will answer.
He will laugh and joke
with me,
then turn serious:

remind me the Arctic sea ice
is still melting,

remind me polar bears
are losing their habitat,

remind me poorer countries
face bigger threats than we do,

remind me Daddy
doesn't believe
   in the climate crisis.

Gizmo weaves through
my legs, barking and barking.

"Please, Maddie,"
Daddy says,
hunching down in front of me.
When did he get here?

"I need you to be strong
for Maman's sake."
Daddy's voice is rough,
his blue eyes more intense than normal.
"I need you to
help us."

Even as Daddy ushers me
into the house, his trembling hands
trying to steer my shoulders,
even as Maman hugs me,

her nose
pink from crying,
even as Aria flings herself onto
the sofa, arms crossed,
face caving in,
the wall in my head grows
harder.

It's Not True

Strum didn't disappear.

Maybe he went hiking and got lost
and now he's wandering around the woods,
thirsty and hungry and confused.

Maybe he went mountain climbing
and twisted his ankle.

Maybe he fell in a hole
and got stuck.

I wrap my arms around
my middle. The cement has
spread from my head to
my stomach, my legs,
everywhere.
My mouth tastes of metal
and I swallow it down.

"Maddie," Daddy says.
"We need your help."

My help? "Why?"
A crack forms
in the cement.
A crack that runs from my head
to my chest.

"A detective is on his way here,"
Daddy says.

Maman wipes her eyes with a balled-up tissue.
"He wants to talk to us," she says.
"He'll need to find out
more about Strum."

Daddy holds my hand in
his rough, unsteady one. "And
you know Strum better than
anyone."

This is true.

Chunk by chunk,
the cement wall
crumbles.

The House Is Too Quiet

The house is too quiet.

It takes me a moment
　　　　but then I realize

there is no music.

Music always fills
our house. Mostly classical music.

Sometimes Daddy plays the piano.
He's a piano tuner by day,
a composer by night
　　　　(not that anyone wants to buy
　　　　his compositions).
Or he plays a vinyl record,
insists it's a warmer, richer sound than digital.

Maman often sings or hums
snatches of operas.
Her voice is warm and soothing,
like having your hair brushed
by someone else.

She's a voice coach
with a tiny studio in town
　　　　(not that anyone here
　　　　wants to learn opera).

Without music
the house is too
unsettling.

The Detective

The detective
lumbers into the living room,
wheezing a bit,
and hikes up his pants.
He's a large man with
small squinty eyes
and closely cropped gray hair.

Maman shows him to
the company chair
(the one where we're not allowed
to sit) and he sinks in.

He accepts a cup of coffee
from Daddy's trembling hands,
hot liquid sloshing
into the saucer.

Gizmo barks up at the stranger.
I murmur into his shaggy hair,
"Gizmo, Gizmo.
It's okay. Quiet now."

The detective smiles briefly at me
—exactly the kind of
fake smile some grown-ups
award to a very small child.
I don't like that kind of grown-up.

But if he can find Strum
I will make an exception.

The Facts

The detective's name is
Michael Sanderson.
He is our liaison
with the Colorado police unit.
In his rumbly bass voice
he repeats the facts of the case.

Strum walked away from campus
at approximately 2:30 p.m.
yesterday,
which was Thursday.
A security camera caught him striding
purposefully across the lawn,
his backpack slung over
one shoulder.
The detective
holds out a phone,
showing us the blurry photo.
It's Strum all right.
Always in a hurry to go
somewhere.

I almost smile, then catch myself.

In the photo, Strum is wearing
jeans and a hoodie

and hiking boots.
His face is a sickly white
under the black daggers of his hair.

Detective Sanderson
tells us Strum was
heading for the north end
of campus.
"Possibly toward the
downtown bus station."

He looks at Daddy.
"As I told you on the phone,
Mr. Lovato,
his roommate
reported him missing
this morning.
And his professors say he didn't show
for classes today.
You mentioned you
weren't expecting him
for four more days."

The detective pauses
to slurp some coffee.
The guzzling sound makes
my stomach twist.
Don't throw up don't throw up don't throw up

He puts the cup and saucer down
on the end table,

wipes his mouth
with the cloth napkin.
"State police followed
the usual protocol
for missing persons under twenty-one.
They talked to his professors and friends,
searched his room,
put a canine unit on the scent.
Unfortunately,
the dog lost the scent in town."

"What does that mean?"
Maman asks in a whisper.

Detective Sanderson looks
at her and the crinkles
in his dark brown face
soften.
"He might have gotten
a lift."
Maman inhales sharply
but I'm not sure why.
What's going on?

"I don't understand."
Maman's voice cracks,
tears well up in her brown eyes.
"Thanksgiving is next week.
He's coming home on the train Tuesday.
It leaves Denver Sunday night."

I've never seen Maman look
so shaky. So lost. So frightened.
I try to swallow the lump in my throat.

But it's stuck.

No Longer a Mountain

Two years ago
Maman's parents died
when the plane taking them
back home to Paris
went down in the Atlantic.
That was a bleak time
for our family.

But Maman
was our mountain of strength.
She consoled the three of us,
stayed focused,
handled the paperwork
with a detached calm.

Now, though,
she seems different.
Fragile as a crushed leaf.
Thin and white as a dandelion puff.

The lump in my throat
melts into sour bile
and I force it down.

Detective Sanderson rubs his chin.
"I'm sorry, Mrs. Lovato.
These things happen. What we need
to figure out is why.
The search of your son's dorm room
turned up his phone, his tablet,
his laptop. But no notes.
Nothing to indicate where
he was going
or if he was suicidal."
Maman gasps.
Presses her fingers to her lips.

The throw-up feeling
comes roaring back.
I bite my lip
and tell myself I will NOT
be sick.

Aria swears under her breath,
a word we're not allowed to say.
But Maman and Daddy don't even notice.

Daddy squeezes one pale trembling hand
with the other.
He looks at the detective.
"So what you're saying
is that Strum *wanted*
to leave. He simply
walked away."

No!
I don't even realize I've

shouted the word
until they all turn to look at me.
Maman says,
faintly,
"Madrigal."
She never calls me that.

My breath is coming in ragged gasps.

I plead with her silently,
It's not true, right?
But she closes her eyes
and massages her pale forehead,
with its V-shaped worry lines.

"Maddie," Daddy says, "it's all right."

It's not all right.
And it never will be.

My stomach lurches
and I run to the bathroom just in time.

In the Bathroom

"Ma chérie." Maman's soothing voice
fills my ears. Calling me dear.
She dabs my forehead with a damp cloth.

I kneel on the floor, leaning
against the cold hard toilet.

She crouches next to me,
smelling of lavender. It's soothing.

The hum of conversation from the living room
sounds far away.
I don't want to go back in there.

Bite my lip.
I will not cry. I will not cry.

Throwing up was bad enough.

They see me as a little girl
anyway.
But I don't *feel* little.

Can't I just go upstairs,
hide in my bed?
Covers over my head?

Just like when I was

little?

When I Was Born

"When you were born...," Maman says.

Her words make me smile
and sit back.

I love this story.
Maman has told it to me
many times.

"Strum didn't want anything
to do with you. Rien." *Nothing.*
"He was almost seven years old
and refused to help."
Maman rinses the cloth
under cold running water
and drapes it across my neck.
It feels good.

"Aria, on the other hand,
was four
and treated you like a live doll.
She wanted to feed you, dress you,
even bathe you!"

She laughs and I smile, trying
to picture Aria as helpful.

"But Strum made a face
whenever I asked him to do
something for you."

She sighs.
"Un enfant têtu."
A stubborn child.
"He complained
about too many girls
in this family.

He begged for a puppy.
That's when Gizmo
came into our lives.
Your father couldn't refuse Strum
anything at that point."

Maman wipes her eyes.
And I realize
it hasn't been that way
for a long time.

Fresh Air

We go into the kitchen.
A sip of ginger ale. Then another.
The cold fizzy liquid strengthens me
going down. I lick my lips.

When Maman decides I'm all right,
that I'm not going to be sick again,
that I don't have a fever,
she says,
"Why don't you go outside
and get some fresh air?"

It's five-thirty and totally dark now.
I stand in the driveway,
hugging myself.
The detective's car is
parked at the curb
under a streetlight.

Daddy's red SUV sits in the driveway
in front of Maman's little gray Toyota.

Daddy's had this SUV all my life.
We've always called it
Big Red.
I place my palm flat
on the cold door.
This car reminds me of Strum.

The Worst Thing

Last August,
Daddy offered
to drive Strum to college
in Big Red.
They'd be in the car together for
three long days.

While Maman and I helped them
load the SUV,
Strum said,
"Dad, when are you going to
get rid of this gas guzzler and
buy an electric car?"

Daddy didn't say anything
for a minute,
while he wrestled a huge duffel bag
into the backseat.
Then he patted the car roof

the way Strum pats Gizmo,
and said,
"I notice you didn't turn down
my offer to drive you."

Strum shook his head.
"I wanted to take the train.
They're more
energy-efficient.
You're the one who insisted on
driving me."

Daddy's eyes narrowed,
his jaw tightened,
and the muscles in his face snapped.
"Then maybe you should
unload your stuff
and figure out
how to get to the train station
all
by
yourself!"

I think Strum would have
done it too,
if Maman hadn't stepped in.
"Boys, boys," she said,
her voice flat.
"Tais-toi."
Surprising us all.
Maman never says
"Shut up."

She shook her head.
"Just as stubborn
as your father," she muttered.
"Comme les deux doigts
de la main."
Like two fingers on the same hand.

Strum reared back
as if she had hit him
but instead of a mark on his skin
the pain was deep inside
his mind.

As if being compared to Daddy
was
the worst thing.

All We Could Fit

When I turned six
we celebrated my birthday
at the Philadelphia Zoo.
I was allowed to invite
three of my kindergarten friends
because that's all we could fit
into Big Red,
along with us five.

Everyone in my family
had a responsibility.

Daddy took pictures,
Maman carried the zoo map,
and Strum and Aria
were supposed to herd
the four kindergartners around.

Aria was ten and happily took charge,
keeping us together,
bossing us around.
"Pay attention, girls," she said.
"This way, girls."
I didn't mind.
None of my friends had older sisters.

But Strum was a few months shy of thirteen
and lagged behind, muttering,
"Wild animals in captivity."

Aria got mad at him. "You're supposed
to be helping me with these kids."
He shrugged and continued to fall behind.

My friends liked grooming
the sheep and goats at the children's petting zoo.

But I liked the leopards and tigers
in Big Cat Falls,
even if Big Cat Crossing was a little scary.
A lion stalked overhead
through enclosed wire trails,
looking mean and powerful.

"At least they get to roam around,"
Daddy said. "Stretch their legs."

Strum just shook his head.
"Caging animals. It's—it's vicious."

Little Sister

I shiver and pull my sweater tighter.
It's too cold out here.
When I duck back into the kitchen,
Maman is not there.
The rise and fall of voices comes
from the living room.

Dragging my feet, I go in,
sink into a chair again.
Pat Gizmo, who licks my cold fingers
with his warm scratchy tongue.
Good old Gizmo.

Aria has just been talking.
Now she hugs one of the throw pillows
Maman embroidered years ago.
Blue and green musical notes
dance across the fabric.

Aria looks at me,
then away.

I wonder what they talked about
while I was being sick.
While I was in the driveway.

Detective Sanderson turns to me.
"So you're the little sister."
I stiffen.
"Tell me about your brother."

Aria coughs. It almost sounds
like laughter.

"I'm *twelve*." I say the words
slowly and loudly,
so this man will understand
I'm not *little*.
"I just haven't had
my growth spurt yet."

The detective raises
one bushy eyebrow and his face
crinkles up more, as if
he's trying not to smile. "Okaaaay."
Heart racing, I swallow,
barely able to believe
I've been so bold.

"*Young lady,* please tell me what Strum does
when he's home."

I'm still trying to understand
that Strum is missing

and this man wants me to tell him
what Strum *does*?
"But…"

"Just answer him, Maddie," Daddy says.
"Please tell him what you know about Strum."

Maybe Aria
already did that.

I tick things off
on my fingers. It must
come out even.

"He builds stuff in the garage.
Like airplane models.
Birdhouses."

I look at the detective.
"The summer I was six and he was thirteen,
he built a go-kart.
We rode it down the hill and crashed
into the Kaplans' parked car.
I lost my front teeth."

Detective Sanderson chuckles.

"No, really. I was bleeding everywhere.
Strum carried me home."

Maman closes her eyes.
Maybe she's remembering

all that blood.
I swallow.

Daddy shifts in his chair.

The detective nods. "I see.
What else does he do?"

I tick off more fingers.
"He runs with Gizmo
to stay in shape.
Plays board games.
And video games."

The detective's eyes open wide.
I think he's about to ask, "What games?"
but instead he says,
"I thought Gizmo was *your* dog?"

Gizmo stands up and barks.
Woof! Woof! Woof!
I murmur into his ear and stroke his head,
warmth humming under
my hand,
until he stops barking.

"He's Strum's dog," I say, my voice
wavering, a *tremolo.*
"But he sleeps
in my room now."

Maman turns away,
sobbing into a tissue.

And I wince,
wishing I could
take it back.

When He's Not Home

"What about
when Strum is *not* home?"
The detective's voice grows quieter,
a *decrescendo.*

"What do you mean?" I ask.

He runs a hand over his bristly hair.
"Did your brother ever text you?
Email you?"

"I don't have a phone yet"
—here I glance at Daddy—
"but Strum emails me all the time.
He sends me links to articles
he wants me to read.
About climate change, and politics."

I sit up straighter.
"He emailed me Tuesday night."

Aria interrupts. "He emailed me
Wednesday morning."

Maman whispers,
"Moi aussi."
Me too.
"He emailed me
Wednesday night."

Daddy says nothing but flinches
as if he's in pain.

The detective's bushy eyebrows shoot up.
"I'll need to see
those messages."

Two Days Before He Disappeared

Strum sent me a link
to an article about
melting Arctic sea ice.

As warming seas thin
the summer sea ice,
eighty percent has disappeared
since 1979.
The article depressed me and I know
my parents wouldn't have wanted
me to read it.
They never want me to read or watch
anything
that makes it hard to fall sleep.

But I sent the link
to my best friend, Emma.
She loves polar bears
and worries about their habitat.

Just like Strum.

I bring my tablet downstairs
and show it to the detective,
who skims through the email,
more interested in the few words
Strum wrote than in the article.

He reads the words aloud.
"M, you should read this article.
It's important. And keep playing,
because music is your
superpower. Remember that.
Hey, thanks for taking care
of Gizmo."

Gizmo looks up and woofs once.
I stroke his shaggy head.
Patting Gizmo gives me courage.

"You should read the article,"
I tell Detective Sanderson.
"It's important. Strum said so."

Sanderson makes notes on a pad.
He peers at Maman.
"And your email from your son?"

But before she can answer,
I plow on, like an *attacca* in music.

"Strum must have headed north
to see the polar bears.
Like in the link.
Before the Arctic sea ice
disappears."

The detective nods.
"Thank you, young lady.
That's certainly a possibility."

At least he's taking me seriously.
He asks permission
to forward the email to himself.

Strum's Email to Maman

Maman shows her phone
to the detective
but reads the email aloud
for the rest of us.

Hers is very short.
"Maman,
remember that trip to
St. Martin four years ago?
That was the greatest."

Her voice catches on
the last word.
I don't know if it's because
Mamie and Papy
were still alive then
or because Strum is
missing.

The Butterfly Farm

I was only eight years old
but I remember that trip.

Mamie and Papy
flew from Paris
and met us there.
We didn't get to see
my French grandparents
very often.

We loved staying
with Mamie and Papy
for a week
in the house they rented.
Strum especially loved it.
He was fifteen then.

Strum swam every day.
He tried paddleboarding
and snorkeling.

He got excited when he saw
the tropical fish
and the birds.
Brown pelicans and
those little yellow and black
bananaquits.
"We should live here,"
Strum said.

He and I both loved
the Butterfly Farm.
La Ferme des Papillons, in French.
It was a ten-minute drive
from the rental house.
Maman's idea, but Papy drove us there.

Strum grinned
as the monarchs
and other butterflies
flitted and danced
around us.

We followed
the curving paths between
flowering trees
inside the screened area.
Both of us liked
the blue morpho butterflies best.
Scientific name: *Morpho peleides.*

They were lively and beautiful
and a brilliant blue.

Shiny blue wings
edged in speckled black.

One fluttered past,
seeming to appear and disappear again.
When it settled on a branch
and went still,
Strum figured it out.

"Look, M," he said.
"When it's not flying,
the blue morpho disguises itself
by closing its wings."

The brown undersides
dotted with eyespots
made a perfect camouflage.
To any predator,
the eyespots said,
"Danger! Keep away!"

"Blue morpho!"
Strum shouted
each time he spotted another one.

"Blue morpho!"
I echoed, giggling.

But then
in the tiny gift shop
after our tour,
we saw walls covered

with framed blue morphos
for sale.

Dead blue morphos.

Strum trudged out to
Papy's rental car
and wouldn't talk
the rest of the day.

What Aria's Email Says

I don't get to hear
what Strum emailed to Aria.
She shows the detective
her phone.
"Don't read it out loud,"
she begs.

The detective studies
the email and then gives her
a long look,
eyebrows arched,
his dark brown forehead
wrinkled with questions.
She shakes her head.

I want to know what's
in that email. I know it's
personal but,

after all,
she knows what mine
was about.

My foot starts jiggling on its own.

Strum's Room

On Saturday morning,
Aria and I watch as a team of detectives
comb through Strum's slope-ceilinged room
over the garage,
wearing thin gloves and
turning everything aside,
leaving it a mess.
I want to yell at them.

My hands itch to straighten the piles
of books and papers and
Popular Science magazines.

Aria shakes her head
as if she knows
what I'm thinking.

I'm still wondering
what Strum emailed to her.
Why wouldn't she
let the rest of us see it?
It's private, yes,

and that's a family rule,
        but
the not-knowing will
drive me
crazy.

As we stand in the doorway,
I beg, "Tell me what was in
Strum's email. Please!"

She stiffens. Inches away from me.
"None of your business."

Gizmo wanders into the room,
nose to the floor, sniffing.
Does Gizmo wonder where Strum is?
Or has he already grown used to
his absence since the end of August?
Detective Sanderson looks up.
"Maddie?
The dog's in our way."

"Come on, Gizmo," I say.
"Let's go for a walk."

Keeping Up

In the summer
before Strum went to college
he and Gizmo ran nearly

every day.
They ran for miles
around the neighborhood.

Strum would return
sweaty and red-faced,
thick dark hair matted
over his blue eyes.
Gizmo would pant and wheeze.

One morning, I asked
if I could come too.
Strum said, "I won't slow down
for you, M.
You have to
keep up."

I was determined to stay
by Strum's side
but after half a mile
my legs ached,
my lungs screamed for air,
my heart pounded so loud
the whole neighborhood
could probably hear me coming.
It wasn't long before
I fell behind.

Strum looked back,
grinned,
but kept going.
Away from me.

At least he always
came back.

Everything We Remember About Strum

Later that afternoon,
Detective Sanderson
requests that we each write down
everything we
remember about Strum.
He gives us yellow legal pads.

I'm fidgety and
I can't breathe,
but I start writing.

     Dear Detective Sanderson,
I write.

    1. Strum's favorite food is sweet potato fries.

    2. He wants to be a wildlife biologist
       because he's always loved animals.

    3. Strum loves death metal music, not classical.

    4. He loves to build things. He even helped Daddy
       finish the room over the garage three years ago.

That was when
they still got along.

5. *His hair is black and his eyes are sky blue, just*
   like Daddy's.
   (Irish eyes, Daddy calls them. Daddy got
   them from Nana, who was Marie O'Hanlon
   before she married Pop-Pop Lovato.)

   Aria and I have Maman's brown eyes
   and dark brown hair.

6. *Strum has freckles across his nose.*

7. *He loves to run.*

8. *His favorite color is cobalt blue.*

   I'll bet even Aria
   doesn't remember that.

Everything We Could Do

Now Maman insists on one thing.
"I'm flying out there. I want
to talk to his roommate,
his classmates, anyone
who may know anything."

This is my strong Maman.
I can breathe again.

"What about your voice students?" Daddy asks.
She wraps her arms
around herself. "I'm taking
a leave of absence.
I've already called them.
My studio is closed."

Detective Sanderson coughs.
"The best thing you can do
is let the police do their job.
We have plenty of people
on the case.
They've interviewed everyone
who knows your son.
We've set up a website
so anyone can enter a tip
anonymously.
We've done everything
we could do."

But Sanderson doesn't know Maman.
She will have her way.
She books a Monday-night flight.

Emma and Her Mother

On Saturday evening,
after the detective leaves,

Emma and her mother
stop by, carrying a huge tray
of dumplings.

Mrs. Chen talks to my parents
in the living room,
while Emma and I sit in the kitchen,
looking at the tray of dumplings
taking up most of the table
between us.

They look gluey and wrinkled
and disgusting.
But I don't say anything.
At first Emma doesn't either.
It's calming,
just being two friends
together.

The silence is like an egg.
      Perfect and whole.
Then she cracks it open.
"I'm really sorry about
your brother," Emma says.

As if he's dead.

I stand up so quickly
my chair falls over
with a loud *thwack*.
"He's not dead!
And I hate dumplings!"

The grown-ups come running.
I don't think I'm shouting
but Daddy bellows,
"Calm down, Maddie!"
His angriest voice,
the one he used with Strum.
Never with me.

Gizmo barks and runs around in circles,
nails clicking on the linoleum,
until Aria drags him outside.

Maman wraps her arms around me
from behind and whispers
that Mrs. Chen put a lot of work
into those dumplings.
"And I'm sure they're
delicious, ma petite."
My little one.

Her warm breath
tickles my ear.
"Besides, you haven't
tried Mrs. Chen's dumplings yet.
How would you know
you don't like them?"

I stare at the wrinkled dumplings,
counting them so I won't be sick.
Eleventwelvethirteenfourteen.

Even number. Good.
Now I'm back
in my safe space.

Daddy's voice lightens from angry to stern.
"You need to apologize
to Mrs. Chen."

Apologizing to someone you've insulted
is the rule in this family.
I gulp. Mutter, "I'm sorry."

Mrs. Chen nods
and says, "It's all right, Maddie.
I know things are difficult
right now."
She turns to Emma.
"We should go."

Emma hasn't said a word.
As they leave the kitchen,
her dark eyes look as round
as kettledrums.

What have I done?

Endangered Species

After they leave,
I stay at the table.

Grip the edge.
Trace the scratches
on the varnished wood.

The first time Emma came to our house,
we sat at this same table
to work on a project together.

That was last year.
Sixth grade.

We had gone to different
elementary schools,
so in sixth grade
our friendship
was something new.
We found each other in orchestra.
We were both learning
how to play our instruments.

That autumn,
a year ago,
we were assigned to do a science report
together
on an endangered species.

Neither of us knew anything about
endangered species.
I brought down my tablet
and we were looking stuff up
when Strum walked in.
He was a senior in high school then.
"Hey, M," he said. "Who's your friend?"

"Oh, this is Emma.
Emma, this is
my brother, Strum."
Pride surged through me,
making me
sit up tall.
I liked having a much-older brother,
a good-looking brother.
With dark spiky hair
and blue eyes.

Emma smiled up at Strum
and he smiled back.

"Hey," he said, laughing.
"It's M and Em."

Emma laughed hard,
as if it was the funniest joke
in the world.

"Ha. Ha," I said.
He smiled at her
but not at me.
I shook my head, sucked in a breath.

Emma leaned forward.
"We have to do a report on an
endangered species," she said,
tugging a lock of her straight dark hair.

"Great topic," Strum said.
"There are so many."

He nodded at her
and my stomach lurched.

Gizmo padded into the kitchen,
lapped at his water bowl. Snuffed.
Strum grabbed a treat for him
from the cupboard.
Gizmo gobbled it down.
Strum patted him, rubbed his head.
Then he looked at Emma again.
"So, have you picked your species yet?"

Emma started to answer but I jumped in.
"No, we haven't. We just started."

Strum shoved his hair back.
"You know, with the climate crisis,
nearly a million species will become endangered.
You could talk about the sea turtle,
the leopard,
the bald eagle.
Or even polar bears."

"Ooo," Emma said. "I love
polar bears. I didn't know they were
endangered."
But she wasn't looking at me.
She was smiling up at Strum.

Leaving me
feeling like

an endangered species.

Day Three

On Sunday morning
I wander down to the kitchen.
Daddy, unshaven and hollow-eyed,
sips coffee at the kitchen table.
Aria shuffles in, eyes half closed,
hair sticking up,
and pours herself a glass of juice.
I nibble on toast.
Can't eat, because
nothing
feels normal anymore.
This is the third day
Strum has been officially
missing.

Maman walks in and
announces,
"Be ready by ten-thirty,
everyone.
We're going to church."
Aria says, "What?"
Daddy squints and scratches
his head.

I'm confused too.
We haven't been to Mass
since Nana Lovato's funeral
three years ago.
I count the toast crumbs
on my plate.

Fivesixseveneightnine.
Not a good number.
The throw-up feeling rises
and I clutch my throat.

"We need to pray...for Strum,"
Maman says, her voice
cracking.
I swallow my last bite
of toast, barely able
to get it down.

When ten-thirty arrives, Aria
refuses to come out of
her room.
Daddy, parked in front of
the TV in our den,
shakes his head.
But I don't want Maman
to be alone.

So I go with her.

Church

The church is half empty,
filled with
the ancient smell of hymnals
and melting wax.

Candles flicker.
Parishioners shift on the hard pews.

The organist plays
an unfamiliar hymn.
During the responsorial psalm,
the lector's voice
quavers up and down.
I stumble over the response,
not used to the words.
But Maman doesn't even open
her mouth.
She seems to be silently
praying.

During the homily, though,
she reaches over and brushes my cheek
with two fingers,
gives me
a small smile.

I try to smile back.
Pretend I wasn't crying.

I can't help thinking
she's leaving us
tomorrow.
And I miss her already.
I want more,
a long squishy hug
like when I was little.

Turning back to the missal,
I search for my place.
The orderliness of the Mass
appeals to me.
But not the uncertain feeling.
Who is listening?

God, I think, *if you're
really there,*
please let Strum come home.

A Splintered Life

Daddy drives Maman
to the Philadelphia airport
late Monday afternoon.

Life splinters
into

      two

j   a   g
       g   e   d

      parts.
            Before Strum disappeared.

After Strum disappeared.

      Our family fragments
into

three

        un   n

           eve

parts.

        Aria and Daddy and me at home.

     Maman in Colorado.

       And Strum who knows where.

I want my family
where they belong.
I want
      everything
in its place.
What if something happens
to Maman?
I imagine the plane crashing,
see the smoky ruins.

I can't breathe until she texts Daddy
that she's arrived
safely.

Alive

We FaceTime with Maman the next evening.
There are dark circles under her eyes
and I can barely hear her.

My stomach
shivers.

"I've talked to everyone,"
she says. "Walked around campus
with his photo all day. Je suis claquée."
I am exhausted. No wonder.

Tomorrow she's holding a press conference
to ask,
beg,
plead
for help from anyone
who may have seen Strum
leave.
"Anyone," she adds, "who may have
seen him
alive."

The word "alive" echoes
inside my head.
Alive, alive, alive.

Be alive, Strum.
Please be alive.

Sleepless

The days
turn into one long gray bleary one,

filled with food from neighbors
and fitful attempts at sleep.

Daddy doesn't mention school
so we don't go.
Maman had already told them
we'd be out for a while.
I miss geometry,
because math is logical.
Calming.
But I don't miss
the high school kids who take it
with me.

I haven't forgotten Strum's email
to Aria. I wish I could find a way
to convince her to show it to me.
Even though it's private.

I will have to wait for
the right moment,
when she is off her guard.

I miss Emma,
but she might
hate me now.
I still need to apologize
for my outburst.

I'm waiting for the right words.

When the words
don't come to me,

I spend hours
straightening and organizing my books
instead.
Pulling them off the shelves
and putting them back
in perfect
order.

That takes me to my safe space.
Calm.
Orderliness.

I can breathe again.

Thanksgiving

Our neighbor
Mrs. Kaplan
comes to the door
the day before Thanksgiving with
another casserole.
She smells of talcum powder.
Daddy asks her in,
but she won't stay.

"I just wanted to invite you all
for Thanksgiving," Mrs. Kaplan says,
patting her already-perfectly-in-place gray hair.
"We'd be happy to cook for you."
She smiles broadly.

How can anyone smile
when Strum is missing?
How can anyone think of eating
Thanksgiving dinner?
There is nothing to give thanks for,
nothing to celebrate.

Strum always loved Thanksgiving.
He looked forward to the holiday.
Looked forward to cranberries
and sweet potatoes in orange cups.
That's why this feels all wrong.
He was supposed to
be home now.

Daddy says,
"Thank you very much, Mrs. K.,
but I think we'll stay
here."

Aria takes the casserole
from a disappointed Mrs. Kaplan
and says, "Thanks."
Another casserole with chicken
and limp vegetables in cream sauce.

My stomach churns.
Maybe I'll have

toast for dinner.

Last Thanksgiving

Last Thanksgiving
started out quietly enough
but then Strum held up his hand
as Daddy carved the turkey.

"None for me, thanks," Strum said.
We all looked at him.
Strum loved turkey.
What was he talking about?

Daddy erupted.
"What do you mean, none for you?"

"I've decided," Strum said,
"to become a vegetarian."
He reached for the tray of
mashed sweet potatoes
in orange halves.

Daddy set down the carving knife,
pointed a finger at Strum.

"You need protein!
And your mother went to
a lot of trouble
to cook this meal.
So you'll *eat* it!"
He bellowed so loud
Aria and I

had to cover our ears.
Maman frowned, looked away.

Strum just shrugged
and filled his plate
with vegetables.
"I don't want to kill
animals anymore."

Daddy stood up and threw down his napkin.
"I have news for you.
Not eating tonight won't bring this bird

back to life."

Last Thanksgiving
made my heart sink,
made me breathless,
made me wish

I were anywhere else.

Every Day

Every day
I go on the website
the detectives set up.

Every day
I look at the photos
of Strum.

Every day
I recount and reread
the updates
on the case.

Every day I wonder
where Strum went.

My Father at the Piano

My father
sits at the piano,
his narrow chin
resting in his left hand,
while the long graceful fingers
of his right hand
pick out a lonely melody.

I watch him from halfway down
the stairs.
Daddy doesn't notice me
but I can see through the foyer
and into most of the living room.

This isn't one of Daddy's own
compositions.
He hasn't worked on them
since Strum disappeared.

He's playing a nocturne,
a theme from

String Quartet No. 2 in D Major
by Alexander Borodin.
It's beautiful and sad
and makes me sigh.

Daddy played this over and over
three years ago
when Nana Lovato died of cancer.
(I never knew Pop-Pop. He died the year
I was born.)
Why is Daddy playing this now?
He doesn't think
Strum is dead, does he?

Strum can't be dead.

I refuse to believe it.

Part Two

ADAGIO

They Never Come Out Even

December is an *adagio,*
slow and mournful,
with feeling.
Like *Adagio for Strings*
by Samuel Barber.
The most haunting piece of music I've ever heard.

Early on Monday morning,
Daddy knocks on my door.
"Time to go back to school!"

I groan and turn over,
clutching the pillow.
"Please, Daddy. No!"
Not now.

He bangs on Aria's door
across the hall.
"One more day!" she wails.

"Come on, girls. It's time.
You can't sit around
every day, all day."

There's a chilly edge to his voice,
like a ribbon of ice clinging
to the banks of Russet Creek.

"I have appointments today,"
he says. "Pianos to tune.
You girls should go back
to school."

At school,
my mind is never on
my schoolwork,
or orchestra
or anything
but Strum.

I count my steps between classes,
hoping they'll come out even.
They never do.

I need even numbers.
Geometry will save me.

Problems Easily Solved

Third period every morning,
I have geometry
at Rachel Carson High School,
down the street from
my middle school.
I always have to rush to get there,
clutching my permanent hall pass.
The high school kids
are a lot taller than I am.

Usually, they ignore me
and I ignore them.

Today, when I come back to class
for the first time in two weeks,
slipping into my seat five minutes late,
as usual,
Nico Torres stares at me
from the next row.
I wish he would stop.
But I'm not bold enough to say anything.
What is his problem?
Mrs. Turner looks up and frowns.
"Mr. Torres, eyes on your own paper."

I turn to the proof
in front of me.
Try to solve it as quickly as possible.
Prove the angles are congruent.
This is easy.
Alternate interior angles
of parallel lines
are congruent.
If only the problem of Strum's
disappearance could be so easily
solved.

It's not fair.

A shiver runs
up my neck and I start counting
the legs of all the desks.

Nice even numbers.
Now
I can breathe.
I'm safe.

Then
someone whispers in my ear,
"How did you do that problem
so fast?"
It's Nico.

Going AWOL

As I'm gathering my things
after class
Nico pauses by my desk.
"Sorry to hear
about your brother
going AWOL," he says.

At least
he doesn't make it sound
as if Strum is dead.

"Thanks," I say, and
try to duck around him,
clutching my book to my chest.

"Your sister is in
my English class,"

Nico adds.
I look up into
his warm brown eyes.

I never realized
Aria knows some of these
kids.

Guess I'm lucky she's
already had
geometry.

Dead Musicians

I head for the door.
Nico follows. "Wait up a sec."

"I have to go," I say.
"Or I'll be late for lunch."

He strides along with me
toward the school entrance.
"I've seen you after school,"
he says, "crossing Union Street with a music case.
What instrument do you
play?"

When I tell him, he smiles
and says,
"I used to play the trumpet.

So what kind of music
is your favorite?"

I keep walking, almost
at the main doors,
freedom only heartbeats away.
"Anything classical,"
I say, steeling myself,
waiting for him to
make fun of me.

"You like dead musicians?"
he asks.

I smile and
point to his shirt
with a faded picture of
Jimi Hendrix.

"I bet you like
Janis Joplin,
Jim Morrison,
John Lennon,
George Harrison,
and David Bowie too.
Six dead musicians."

His thick eyebrows arch
and his light brown face
splits into a huge grin.
"You're okay, muchachita."

I squinch up my face.
"What does *that* mean?"

Nico shrugs, his dark eyebrows waggling.
"It just means...like, little girl.
It's what my grandmother calls my sister.
She's six."

I sigh.
Another person who thinks of me
as a little girl.

The Longer You Wait

Our end of the table is an island of quiet
in the hurricane of seventh-grade lunch.

Someone drops a tray and
the clang of dishes echoes
through the room.
Kids shriek and laugh.
Too loud.
Somehow, Emma manages to ignore it.
She's the calmest person I know.

I huddle in my seat.
First, I unwrap my sandwich quarters.
Then I arrange the quarters
exactly one thumb-width apart.

Then I eat them.
Chewing slowly.
Making the bites come out even.

Emma doesn't mention
my rudeness
over the dumplings.
I'm kind of surprised
she even saved me a seat at our usual table.
But she doesn't talk to me.
She doesn't perch on the edge
of her seat and lean forward
to tell me
about melting Arctic sea ice or
what's happening to the polar bears.

Something aches in the middle
of my chest.
I miss her talking. I miss
her polar bear news.

And I need to tell her I'm sorry.
Why did I wait so long?
The longer you wait to apologize
the harder it becomes.

Between Us

This awkwardness between us will not end.
If I don't speak up soon, I'll lose my friend.

A Secret

I put down my second sandwich quarter.
"Em-Emma."
The words catch in my throat.
"That day with the dumplings."
And I look at her.
"I shouldn't have yelled at you.
I'm sorry. Really sorry."

"That's okay," she says.
"You were hurting."
She leans in.
"Maddie,
I'll tell you a secret."
She lowers her voice.
"I don't like dumplings either."

We both crack up laughing.

It feels good to laugh,
shaking with a lively *allegro* beat.
Then I catch myself
and go rigid,
curling my hand into a fist,
nails digging into my palm
so I'll feel the pain.
How can I laugh
when Strum is still
missing?

Emma doesn't notice
me stiffening.

Or maybe
she pretends not to.

I look around again at the chaos.
The kids at the other end
of the table
are laughing.

I frown.

Wait. Is Topher smirking at me?

One Small Pink Flower

"Is there any news?" Emma asks.
"About your brother?"
I shake my head and go back
to eating.

Topher
laughs with his friends,
his thin brown hair falling
in his eyes.
I turn my head more toward Emma
and block him out.

"I've been wanting to tell you,"
Emma says, sounding wistful.
She twirls a lock
of her hair.

"Our rhododendron bush
has a bloom. One small
pink flower."
I look at her, puzzled.

"It's December," she says.
"It already bloomed in May.
But it's been so warm,
a flower
popped out.
See?"
She holds up her phone
and I peer at the photo.

What does this small pink flower
have to do with Strum?

Inside my head
I hear the ominous music
of the French horns
from *Peter and the Wolf*
and I want to scream.
Something simmers inside me,
threatening to boil over.
But I can't let it.
Not again.
I concentrate on my last sandwich quarter
and count the bites.
One two three four.

"It's climate change," Emma says,
sure of herself, as always.

I wish I could be that sure
of things.
I wish I knew
where to look for Strum.

Turkey, Lettuce, and Tomato

Every day I eat the same lunch.
Maman made it for me until
I turned twelve last April
and started making it
myself.

Turkey, lettuce, and tomato
on whole wheat bread,
spread
with just a little mayo
so it doesn't squirt out
the sides.

Saliva fills my mouth
whenever I even think
about it.

Now
Topher
watches me
chew.

Creep.

What Topher Must Be Thinking

We have to be nice
to you
because your brother
disappeared.

We have to be nice
to you
because your family
is troubled.

We have to be nice
to you
because you are a math nerd.

I am 98 percent sure
this is what goes through his head
when he looks at me.

I'd like to splash my milk
in his face.

The Word "Club" Makes Me Cringe

While we walk to
orchestra rehearsal,
Emma begs me
to join Eco Club.

"You can do both, you know.
Orchestra *and* Eco Club.
We meet during free period
on Wednesdays. So you
wouldn't be missing anything."

Free period is when I escape to
the back corner of the library.
The quietest spot to read.
"Maybe," I say.
But I'm just being polite.
I'm really thinking
no, never.

The Idea for Eco Club

Emma got the idea
for Eco Club
from Strum.

That was the second time
she came to my house,
while we worked more on our report.

Strum said,
"When you girls are in high school
you should join the Environmental Club."
He grinned.
"I started it, you know, Emma."

My mouth tasted like copper.
Why was he showing off?
I cringed when
Emma smiled up at him.
"What do you do?" she asked.

He tilted his head.
"We've taken field trips
to wetlands,
planted trees,
held protests.
Mostly we try
to raise awareness
about carbon dioxide and methane.
Tell people countries like ours
produce the most carbon
while underdeveloped countries
suffer the effects.
Make posters, have assemblies,
stuff like that."

It sounded like a lot of work to me.
And I knew what Daddy always said
about climate change.

But Emma looked enchanted.
"Yeah, that would be great! Wonder why
we don't have a club like that
at our school."

Strum shrugged.
And then smiled his biggest smile.
"Maybe you'll have to start one."

Why would Strum tell Emma
to start a club like that?
Why not me?

Sitting Next to Oliver

At orchestra rehearsal,
I sit next to Oliver.

Oliver is the first oboist
and I am the second.

Oliver is an eighth grader.
He always wears a crisp button-up shirt.
His thick blond hair looks
just combed.

Sitting next to Oliver
makes me feel like I'm in kindergarten.
Like I should brush my messy hair
and fix that rip
in my jeans.
I tuck my feet under the chair
to hide the scuff marks
on my sneakers.

Sometimes Oliver and I play together,
both oboes in concert,
which means at the same time.
Side by side.

The same notes.
But sometimes Oliver plays alone.

Oliver is fantastic.
If I could be as good as Oliver,
Mr. Dahlberg would give me
a solo.

I know he would.

When Oliver Plays

When Oliver plays,
I keep still and listen.
What is it Oliver can do
that I can't?

When Oliver plays,
he produces more feeling.
I hear it in the sweet shimmering
notes from his oboe.

When Oliver plays,
my insides press against my rib cage,
my throat crackles, my eyes sting.

When Oliver plays,
there is only the pure joy of
music.

Feelings

Why can't I play like that?
Am I some kind of
machine
that plays by rote,
producing perfect notes with
no feeling?

What about all these
confused feelings
I've been keeping bottled up
inside?
Mostly about Strum,
but also Aria and Maman and Daddy?
And the world?
What if I could
really listen to those feelings?
What if I could discover a way
to let them out?

I go home and practice
until my lips burn.
I will not
stop.

The Duck's Theme

Strum said this music made his body hum.
The more I play these notes, the more I feel
as if I'm reaching out and calling Strum.

Opening the Door

Daddy puts a casserole
in the microwave
and I set the table,
lining up the forks and knives
equal distances apart.
They have to be perfect.
I fold a cloth napkin into
a crisp triangle
at each place.

Aria is still upstairs.
If she doesn't come down soon
Daddy will yell.
We have rules in this house.
Everyone comes to dinner.
No exceptions.

The silence between Daddy and me
seems to suck all the air
out of the kitchen.
I wonder what to talk to him about.
Then I remember what Emma said today.
I take a deep breath.
"Daddy, can I ask you something?
Is it…I mean,
do you know why Emma's
rhododendron has a bloom?
In December?"

He raises his eyebrows at me
without speaking

and for the first time
I notice
his dark brows are peppered with gray.
When did that happen?

"Emma says
the world is getting warmer
and it's our fault. Humans."

Daddy shakes his head,
chuckles a little.
"That's nonsense, Maddie.
A hoax.
Don't listen to her."

Humph.
I clench my fists,
wanting to shout,
It's not nonsense. It's true!
If I were brave,
I would say it.

Instead,
I turn my back on him
and open the cupboard door
to get the water glasses.

By the time Aria comes downstairs,
I'm calm again.

After Dinner

My sister is sketching while propped up in bed.
Her door is half open, so I slip inside.

She looks up and sees me. A scowl fills her face.
"I'm *busy*," she tells me. "Now please go away."

There are four years between us. A cavernous gap.
It's so wide I don't think I'll ever cross over.

I shuffle one foot on the threadbare gray rug.
And whisper, "It's just ... I was wondering what ..."

"Don't mumble," she orders. "Mad, what do you need?"

"I just want to know. What did Strum's email say?"

She leaps up and shoves me out into the hall.
"It's none of your business! Get out of my room!"

She slams the door shut and the sound hurts my ears.

My sister's been shutting me out for years.

Aria's Room

Aria's room used to be my room too.

That was before Strum and Daddy
finished the slope-ceilinged room over the garage.

Back then,
Strum lived in
what is now my room.

Aria and I
shared her room until she was thirteen
and I was nine.

Sometimes it still feels like
my room.
Like I should be allowed to walk in
whenever I want.

Back then,
we used to get along.

Back then,
she would hum bits of songs
while brushing her long hair.

Back then,
she would motion me over
to sit next to her on her bed
and she would brush my hair too.

I loved the warm sleepy feeling
of having my hair brushed
by someone else.

My eyes fell closed every time.

The way she hummed bits
of her favorite songs

reminded me of Maman's
humming and singing.

The songs, of course,
were different.

A Strange New Kind of Normal

The next evening,
just when we are growing used to
a strange new kind of normal,
the three of us,
eating casseroles and frozen dinners,
always behind on laundry
and homework,
Maman calls.

This time,
she will only speak
to Daddy.

But I lean close and
hear her crying on the phone.
Her voice drips with exhaustion.
My heart does flip-flops.
I'm scared.

Gizmo barks up at us.
I stroke his head over and over
to calm him.
Patting Gizmo calms me down too.

"No one knows anything,"
Maman is saying.
"No one knows why he would take off
with no word, no note.
Hunter, je ne sais pas quoi faire d'autre."
I don't know what else to do.

My throat tightens.
I want to reach through the phone
and feel her arms
around me.

Daddy shifts the phone to his other ear.
"Valerie, come home. Please."

I can hear her clearly now
because she is shouting.
"Non! Absolument pas!"
Absolutely not.
"I'm not leaving without
some word, some hope.
Something!"

Horrible Thoughts

On Wednesday, Daddy flies to
Denver, where Maman
will pick him up in her rental car.

What if something happens?

I push aside more horrible thoughts of
planes crashing.
I wish he didn't have to go.
Or that I could have gone with him.

Now it's just Aria and me.
And we are a discord.

"I think they've maxed out their credit card,"
Aria says. "For flights and hotels and stuff.
And Dad only gave me
two hundred dollars for food.
So it has to last."

Angry Portraits

That afternoon
I peek into Aria's room
and she's drawing again,
furiously sketching with quick
dark strokes in charcoal.

Loud growling music
roars from her phone,
making my head hurt.
There are ripped sheets of paper
taped to the walls
at odd angles.
Every picture
is a portrait of Strum.

Even though the crookedness
makes me cringe,
I have to count the portraits
before she sees me.
I have to count them so
Maman and Daddy
won't disappear too.
Seveneightnineteneleven.
Not a good number.

But she's working on number twelve.

Aria is talking to herself.
"Why?" she says.
Then louder,
"*Why* didn't you
take me
with you?"

For the first time, I realize
Aria could be hurting too.

Leftovers

Aria and I eat a silent dinner
of warmed-up leftover chicken
with bitter overcooked broccoli
in some kind of gooey sauce.
The last of the casseroles.
I think this one was from

the Kaplans.
The empty casserole dish with
its stuck-on bits makes
my stomach hurt.

Aria and I are leftovers.
We are what remained
when Strum disappeared
and first Maman and then Daddy
flew to Colorado.

My throat prickles
from trying so hard
not to cry.
I'm afraid the tears will spill over
anyway.

Aria and I clean up silently,
leaving the big dish to soak.
Gizmo sniffs around
our ankles.
Glad of the excuse
to hide my face,
I lean over to give him a treat.
Aria announces,
"I'm going out. Don't wait up
for me."

On a school night?
"Where are you going?" I ask,
but she just
laughs.
"Out with friends."

People are always leaving me.

Inside my head,
the French horns roar.
I tug my hair
until my scalp burns.

"Don't leave,"
I beg.

She shakes her head,
her dark hair swishing.
"Mad,
it's time for you
to grow up."

Tell Me

"Please,"
I say,
as Aria slips into
her coat.
"If you're going to
leave me alone,
at least tell me
what was in
Strum's email."

She grabs her purse
and opens the door.

"Mad, you need to learn
to mind your own
business."

Stuck

If Aria's going to
leave me alone
all night,
I will
hack into her email.
I open her laptop and try
a few obvious passwords.
Her birthday.
Her favorite book.
Her favorite band.
Nothing works.

Finally
I look at her drawings
still taped to the walls
at crazy angles. Shuddering,
I lean in and peer at them closely.
Each one is signed "AL."
Aria Lovato.
And I have an idea. *ALdraws.*

It works.
Quick as a butterfly,

I scroll through emails
until I find what I'm
looking for.
Strum sent Aria
a link to an article
about Frida Kahlo,
a Mexican artist
known for her
self-portraits.
The words he typed,
though,
shock me with
their harshness.

"I know Dad and Maman
drive you crazy. They drive
me crazy too.
I don't want to be around them
anymore.
Not with their politics.
Not with Dad's stupid rules
and his yelling.
Sorry you're stuck with them
for now.
But just think,
in two years
you can go away to art school.
You'll be free.
Hang in there.
You can do this, A.
I believe in you."

When I exit her email
and close the laptop,
I glance around, as if
someone is watching.

Why does Strum
hate the rules so much?
I *like* the rules. They keep us safe.

Why does Strum
hate our parents so much?
He thinks Aria is stuck with them.
But now I'm the one who feels stuck,
like I'm in the middle of the stairs
and can't go up or down.
I can't tell Maman and Daddy
what Strum said
because then they'll know
what I did.

How could I do that?

I know it was wrong.
I know I broke the rules.
I know I shouldn't have done it.

What kind of horrible person
am I?
Maybe I really am
something mechanical,
without feelings.

Night Sounds

I don't like
being alone at night.
I don't like the dark.
I don't like
the noises the night makes.

Gizmo's with me, of course,
all fur and wag and pant.
For a while we play tug-of-war
with an old chew toy.
Finally, I let him win.
I pet him and bury my face
in his scruffy neck,
breathing in the warm, yeasty smell
of dog.
Inside my head, I hear Strum's voice.
"Gizmo, Gizmo.
It's you and me, buddy."

But after Gizmo curls around and around
and settles down to gnaw on the toy,
I hear the noises
again.

A creaking sound
as the old house groans in the wind.

A scraping sound
as pine branches scratch against siding.

A growling sound
as the refrigerator kicks on.

Three scary noises, but at least I recognize them.

Then there is a *thump thump*
I don't recognize.
What *was* that noise?

I try to call Aria
but she doesn't answer.
I almost call Maman or Daddy.
He should be arriving in Colorado
by now.
But I don't want to worry them.
They're nearly two thousand miles away.
What can they do?

I think about calling Emma.
But Emma lives on the other side
of town and I can't expect her mom to drive
all the way over here
just because I'm scared of the dark.

Instead, I check the locks
on every door.
Then I check them
again.
And again.
And again.

I lie awake for hours,
thinking of Strum going missing.

Maman and Daddy leaving.
Even Aria leaving me tonight.

Leaving

No one should have to handle all this grieving.
Nana Lovato died when I was nine.
I'm twelve years old and people still are leaving.

It's been two years since that distressing evening
Maman found out her parents' plane was down.
No one should have to handle all this grieving.

When Mamie and Papy died, I stopped believing.
And Strum called all those deaths a painful sign.
I'm twelve years old and people still are leaving.

Now Strum is gone and I have trouble breathing.
He walked away without a note, a line.
Can I be mad at Strum and still be grieving?

The missing never know who they're deceiving.
Themselves? Or all of those they left behind?
I'm twelve years old and people still are leaving.

Our parents left us here and I'm not sleeping.
And Aria and I fight all the time.
No one should have to handle all this grieving.
I'm twelve years old and people still are leaving.

Aria at Midnight

I drag Gizmo's flannel-lined dog bed
from my room
downstairs
into the living room,
counting each thump on the steps.
Thumpthumpthump...
Thirteen. Not a good number.
Something bad will happen.

While Gizmo snores,
I doze fitfully
in Daddy's big brown chair,
my puffy blue comforter tucked around me.

Then...
the scritch of a key
in the front door lock.
Gizmo snuffles.
The key jiggles more urgently.

Now
I'm wide awake
and my heart is pounding *prestissimo.*
Gizmo lifts his head and barks.
I leap up as
Aria stumbles through
the front door.
Sees me.
Laughs.

I cross my arms and glare at her.
"It's after midnight!"

Aria doubles over laughing.
"Oh, Mad, you're a hoot.
You should see yourself.
Like a little Maman."
She steps around me
and a strong sweet odor
wafts from her hair,
her knitted sweater.
Red lines web the whites of her eyes.
That sweet smell—
is that what I think it is?
Is Aria high?

Now I don't feel
so guilty
for peeking at her email.
"You should have thought
about me, alone here!
Where did you go?"
Spit flies out of my mouth.

I'm shouting, but she doesn't seem
to notice. Simply
shrugs. Says faintly,
"None of your business."

I kneel down and wrap my arms
around Gizmo's neck.
"I was scared,"
I murmur into his scruffy fur.

She giggles.
"You sound so funny
like that."

I go upstairs to bed but
my light stays on all night.

Come Home Soon

The next evening,
I FaceTime with Maman and Daddy,
without telling them what Aria did.
I'm not a snitch. I don't tell them
how she might have spent
the grocery money.
(For dinner tonight we had
canned soup.)
But I'm still angry with her.
And a little scared.

"There was a thumping noise
last night," I tell them.

Daddy smiles. "Relax, Maddie.
It's the heater starting up."

"Come home," I tell them. "Now.
Please. I need you here."
I lean close to the screen,
hoping they'll see the worry
etched into my face.

"Soon," Daddy says. "We're
following up
on a possible lead.
A highway worker
thinks he saw Strum
near Billings, Montana.
You may have been right.
Strum may have headed north."

"Come home," I beg again.

"We will," Maman says,
and then she leans in and adds softly,
"Tu me manques aussi,"
I miss you too.
Responding to the words I
didn't say.

My eyes sting.

"Tomorrow?" I ask. "Will you
fly home tomorrow?"

Daddy rubs his face.
"A few more days, Maddie.
Then we'll both be home.
Try not to worry so."

I will
count the hours.

Play for Us

Maman asks me to
play something for them.
"I miss the sound of
your oboe, ma petite."

I open my music case
and assemble the instrument,
thinking of Strum.
Maybe he really did head north
to see polar bears.

First, I play the duck's theme
from *Peter and the Wolf.*
Trying to call Strum home.

Then I play "Largo" from *Symphony No. 9*
by Antonín Dvořák.
The first piece Mr. Rimondi
taught me and
one of the few pieces
I've learned by heart.
It calms me. Maybe it will
calm Maman too.

On the screen, Maman dabs her eyes,
but she is smiling.
Daddy nods in time as I play,
his eyes closed.

Then I remember Daddy has an old record
of Paul Robeson singing

"Goin' Home," which is
based on "Largo."
I didn't choose the song on purpose
to make them
want to come home.

Or maybe I did.

Foreign Object

On Friday morning,
I decide I will go back to music lessons,
making Aria promise
four times
that she won't forget
to pick me up
at four-thirty.
She clamps her lips together,
as if to keep cruel words
from escaping.

I haven't been to Mr. Rimondi's
for three weeks.

On Friday afternoon,
as I put my oboe together,
it feels like a foreign object
in my hands.
I've forgotten my best reed,
and this backup reed is

no good.
How can I even play?

Fragile

"Come on, Madrigal.
You can do this,"
Mr. Rimondi says.
"Let the music help."

I frown as I
slide the reed
between my lips.
Before I realize
what I'm doing
I've bitten down on
the heart of it.
The twin pieces of cane
crack
right down the spine
with a tiny crunching sound.
I pull out the splintered reed
and stare at it.

Everything falls apart.

Tears well up in my eyes
and threaten to spill over.
The notes on the sheet music
wave and bend.

I don't want to cry
in front of Mr. Rimondi.
But
my family has become
an oboe reed,
fracturing into shards.

We are
the duck
swallowed by the wolf
in Prokofiev's tale.

We are melting
Arctic sea ice.

Mr. Rimondi Tries to Fix It

"Tell you what,"
Mr. Rimondi says,
his voice higher than normal,
chirpy and bright.
"You can try out one of my new
super-special handmade reeds.
You can be my tester.
All right, Madrigal?"
He's treating me
like I'm five years old.
I don't know whether to
laugh or cry.

He smiles. "I have no idea
if they even work. Someone
needs to test one."

I nod,
staring at the
tiny wrinkles around his eyes,
concentrating on keeping
tears from spilling out of my own.
When he turns away to search
through the stacks on his desk
for the reed case,
I wipe my eyes
with the back of my hand
twice, quickly.

The new reed is smooth and
tastes raw
and makes my oboe sound
better.
But even Mr. Rimondi
with his laugh lines
and new reeds
can't fix what's broken
in my family.

Walking in the Woods

Early on Saturday morning,
I take Gizmo for a walk

in the woods
behind our neighborhood.
Stepping over logs
and crunching through
brown leaves.

I count my steps until Gizmo
stops to sniff.
"What do you think, Gizmo? Will they ever
find Strum?"

I crouch down,
hug his shaggy neck.
Gizmo looks around,
licks my face.
Tail wagging like a metronome.

"He's going to be okay, right?"
He barks. Sometimes I wish
Gizmo could talk.

But at least in the woods I can talk to him without
anyone hearing.

Nobody ever comes to this small
community park except me.
Especially now. It's the dead time
of year.

Everything is brown and dry,
except that one pine tree.

Cardinal

Cardinal perches
on the topmost pine tree branch.
Bright red question mark.

Heroes

Walking in the woods always
reminds me of Strum.
Henry David Thoreau
used to be one of his heroes.
Strum loved a line in Thoreau's essay "Walking."
"In wildness is the preservation
of the world."

After we visited Concord, Massachusetts,
two summers ago
and saw the reconstructed cabin,
Strum wanted to build his own simple hut
in the woods.
"I'm going to live off the land,"
he said.

But later Strum learned
that the entire time
Henry David lived
at Walden Pond,
he took his dirty laundry
home to his mother.

Strum told me he didn't admire
Thoreau anymore after that.

Now that I know what Strum
thinks of our parents,
I'm torn between sadness
and anger.
Why did you go away?
I scream silently,
wanting to hit something.
Wanting to hit Strum.

It's hard
for me to admit
but
Strum
may not be
the person I thought
he was.

Saturday Night

Emma invites me to a
sleepover.
I hate sleeping in a different bed.
But I say yes,
because Maman and Daddy
tell me I should
when I call them to ask.

(I'd been hoping they would
say no.)

Aria says, "Go and have fun.
I'll be here with Gizmo."
She's being far too friendly,
which makes me suspicious.
What is she up to?

Mrs. Chen and Emma
come to pick me up before dinner
in their electric car.
"Should I bring my oboe?"
I ask. I want to keep practicing
the oboe solos
from *Peter and the Wolf.*
Emma squinches up her face.
"Why would you want
to bring that?
We're going to watch movies
and paint our nails."

I hide my hands
with their short raggedy nails
behind my back
and quickly count the stripes
on Emma's socks.
Four black stripes, four white stripes.
This makes me laugh.
I point to her ankles.
"You look like a zebra."

Emma looks down at her socks and giggles.
Maybe this sleepover won't be so bad
after all.

Mrs. Chen drives hunching forward,
both hands
gripping the wheel tightly.

The car crosses over Russet Creek
and I'm careful to avoid
looking at the falling-down
building to the right
of the bridge.
It makes me too jittery.

The First Time I Saw Emma's House

The first time I saw Emma's house,
a small one-story house
in a more crowded neighborhood than ours,
was on a Saturday nearly a year ago.
When we worked more on the science project
together.

I was astonished at how small
her house was.
How tired it looked,
despite being spotlessly clean.

But I didn't say anything.

Back then, I didn't stay overnight.
And I remember how glad I was
to go home again.

In Emma's Room

We stash my stuff
on the extra bed
in Emma's room.

Posters
of polar bears
cover the walls
in Emma's room.

There are messy piles
of books and papers
and old toys
in Emma's room.

My fingers tingle.
I want to straighten
everything
in Emma's room.

The Trouble with Onions

While we're in Emma's room,
in the back corner of this small house,

I smell onions frying.
Onions sizzling in butter
might be the most
delicious smell in the world.
I close my eyes and
breathe deeply.

But the trouble with onions is
when Daddy cooks them
it means meat loaf.
Meat loaf is *not* my favorite.

I count the posters on Emma's walls.
Onetwothreefourfive.
Not a good number.
"Are we having meat loaf?"
I ask Emma.
She shakes her head, smiling.
"We don't eat beef.
Cows produce
a lot of methane
and that's bad for the environment.
You should know that.
Strum knew—" She winces.
"I mean, Strum knows that."

I nod.

Dinner turns out to be
fish with lemon and onions.
And broccoli on the side.

I discover
even broccoli tastes good
with lemon and onion sauce.
Aria and I have been living on
canned spaghetti and tuna.

Mrs. Chen eats with chopsticks
but Emma doesn't.
So I don't either.

Emma's Father

I've never asked Emma
about her father and how he died.
I only know that
he died a long time ago.

Back in Emma's room
after dinner,
I ask, "Do you still
miss your father?"

She opens a drawer,
shows me a picture of a smiling man.
"I don't really remember him,"
she says. "Just that he smelled like limes.
I was only three
when he was killed
in a car accident."

I close my eyes and breathe.
One two three four deep breaths.
"Emma, I'm really sorry."

No wonder
Mrs. Chen gripped the steering wheel
so tightly.

Homesick

I want to hang out and have fun.
But I can't.
I can't help fidgeting.
As Emma arranges different colors
of nail polish on the dresser,
I pace her small room
back and forth,
back and forth,
counting to myself,
onetwothreefour.
Four paces.
That's all it takes to get across the room.

Strum would love her polar bear posters.
But
her room is too messy
and I want to put
everything in its place.

Emma is familiar with
my pacing (though my counting

is a secret).
I've paced across
her room
before.

"What color do you want?"
she says.
I don't want to
paint my nails.
I just want to be home
in my own neat, organized room
—my room that used to be Strum's—
snuggled up next to Gizmo
and reading a book.

"Emma," I say.
"I want to go home."

She tilts her head.
"Really? I mean,
we don't have to do nail polish."
She doesn't sound
so sure of herself
anymore.
She pushes the bottles back
with lots of clinking.
"I just thought that's what
girls
are supposed to do
on sleepovers."

"Who knows?"
I shrug.

"I've never
been on one."

She giggles. "Me neither."

"Ha!" I smile. "We're so popular."

Emma grins. "I know, right?
We're totally the hottest kids in school."

We bubble over in cascades of laughter,
collapsing on the floor
and laughing until we're weak.

It feels good to laugh
and this time I don't stiffen with guilt.
I miss Strum, but not laughing
won't bring him back.

Besides, I'm still kind of angry with him.

After a while, we sit up and talk.
I tell Emma my theory
about Strum and the polar bears
and she nods as if
it makes perfect sense.
After all, she's surrounded by them.

Then she changes
the subject.
"You're so lucky you get to sit
next to Oliver in orchestra.
Do you like him?"

"He's okay."

"I'm hoping to convince him
to join Eco Club," she says.
And there's a faraway look
in her eyes that makes me
bite back a smile. "You too, of course,"
she adds quickly.

It's fine, I want to say.
I don't really want to join
your club, I want to say.

I don't say it.

Instead I say, "I'm thinking about it."

Being with Emma is fun.
But after a while
I look around her small room
with its polar bear posters.
My stomach tightens
and my mouth is dry.
"Emma, I still want to go home.
I'm sorry. I just...
miss it."

"You're homesick for your house?"
This is why she's my best friend.
She understands.

Driving Home

I use Emma's phone to call
home for a ride
but
Aria doesn't answer.

Mrs. Chen drives me home
without a word.
Emma comes along for the ride.
"Thank you for dinner, Mrs. Chen,"
I say. "It was very good."

Finally, she nods. "Glad you enjoyed it."
Her hands grip the wheel again,
knuckles pushing against skin
like butterflies trying to climb out
of their chrysalises.
I'm sorry Mrs. Chen has to drive me
home in the dark
when she doesn't even
like to drive.

I count pairs of headlights
on the other cars we pass.
Fivesixseveneight.
Good. We'll be safe.

On the way home,
we cross Russet Creek again.
This time I can't help looking
at the falling-down building,
though it's too dark

to see much.
The glint of moonlight
on a jagged piece of
corrugated tin roof,
shards of glass,
a door hanging
sideways.

Decay

Decay
fascinates and horrifies me
at the same time.

I don't mean decay in nature.
A crumbling log has
its own kind of beauty.
Mushrooms cluster on the bark.
Ants bore through it.
The log breaks apart
into rust-colored chunks
that smell damp and earthy
and feel as soft as fabric
washed a thousand times.

Tiny white flowers
will push through the dead leaves
under the log
in spring.
That is the way of nature.

No, it's not nature that disgusts me
but the decay of
buildings.
The old artist's studio
clings precariously
to the banks of Russet Creek.
I don't know how long
it's been there,
decades probably.
Maybe a century.
But it's falling apart.
Gaping holes bloom in the roof,
the windows are smashed in,
the floor slants dangerously
toward the water.

The old studio is a giant
missing most of his teeth
and dangling two broken arms.
It's ugly.
Off-kilter.
Embarrassing.

There is nothing beautiful
about this once-sturdy
building falling apart.
Nothing inspiring about
the rust and ruin of metal
and wood and glass.

My family
is beginning to resemble

the crumbling studio
on Russet Creek.
We are

f
a
l
l
i
n
g

a   p   a   r t.

The Riot of Music

I say goodbye and thanks
to Emma and her mother,
then let myself in the front door.

Gizmo barks and barks
from the basement,
muffled compared to
the riot of music
from the living room.
An angry metal song blasts from
Daddy's stereo
like a growling beast.
No wonder Aria didn't hear
my phone call.

Aria and three of her friends
are in there.
There's a couple I don't know,
the girl sitting on the guy's lap
in Daddy's chair.
But the fourth person is
Nico Torres.
He's squeezed in with Aria
in the company chair.
Nico sits up, waves at me,
shouts over the song.
"Hey, it's the math genius!"

Aria just stares at me,
as if I'm a total stranger.
She's holding a thick brown bottle
and a sour odor fills the room.

If I were brave, I'd tell these kids
get out,
go away,
this is my house too!
If I were brave, I'd tell Aria
you're not allowed to sit
in the company chair and
you know it.
But I'm not brave.

Nico gets up and turns off the music
and the sudden silence pulses in my ears.

"Er, Aria, maybe we shouldn't
be doing this," Nico says.

"You're in charge
of your little sister."
He pries the bottle from
Aria's hand, takes it into the kitchen.
The splash of liquid in the sink
echoes in the quiet.

Nico must have opened the basement door,
because Gizmo comes huffing into the room,
licks my hand, huddles against me,
shivering.
Me too, Gizmo. Out of our element.
My throat stings.
I'm determined not to cry.

The other guy and girl
shift in their seat, break apart.
She stands up and grabs her purse.
He rubs the back of his neck.
"We better get going. See you later, Aria."
The door slams after them.

I count the empty beer bottles littering the floor.
Onetwothreefourfivesixseven.

Finally, Aria shakes her head at me.
"What are you doing here? You're
supposed to be staying at Emma's."

I stare back
and realize this is a
different Aria
from the one I grew up with.

Why did she lock up Gizmo? Why was she drinking?

Where did Aria go when Strum disappeared?

High Five

At lunch on Monday
I tell Emma about Aria's
Saturday-night party.
"They were drinking beer," I whisper,
wrinkling my nose.

"Ugh," Emma says. "I'm never going
to do that."

I giggle. "It smelled pretty bad."

"Bet it tastes worse," Emma says,
laughing.

At the other end of the table
Topher is giving me looks.
I count the cracks in one floor tile.
Seveneightnineten. Good.

When I look up he's still staring.
"What?" I say to him.
He flinches, turns pale.

"Wow! He didn't expect you to speak up,"
Emma says.

She slaps me a high five
and I grin.

Trying Too Hard

No matter how hard I try
I can't put enough feeling
into the notes of the duck.
I try before rehearsal officially starts,
hoping Mr. Dahlberg,
who is shuffling through sheet music,
will hear me and be impressed.
But trying too hard
only makes me miss the notes.
Squeak. Kraark. Squeal.

Mr. Dahlberg
taps his music stand.
Onetwothree taps.
"If you've finished tuning up,
Ms. Lovato, perhaps the rest of us
can now begin."

My face burns and my heart
jumps around in my chest.
Now Mr. Dahlberg will never
give me that solo.
Emma sends me an encouraging smile
from the clarinet section,
but

Oliver looks at me sideways,
his eyebrows disappearing
under his perfect hair.

Maybe

Maybe if I learn to play the oboe parts
with *feeling,*
Strum will come home.

Maybe if I get along better with Aria,
Strum will come home.

Maybe if I stop counting everything,
Strum will come home.

Maybe.

At Last

Maman and Daddy are home!
I hug them and won't let go,
drinking in their taste,
their smell. Daddy's musky scent
and Maman's cloud of lavender.
Daddy's stubbled cheeks
and Maman's smooth skin.

"Thankyouthankyouthankyouthankyou
for coming home.
Don't ever leave again."

"If anything happens," Daddy says,
"we will have to leave again.
But there's been no sign,
no word,
no new discoveries."

Which means,
I guess,
Strum's disappearance
continues to be a
mystery.

Christmas

Our parents
make a show of pretending to enjoy
Christmas Day.

Tchaikovsky's *Nutcracker Suite*
plays on the stereo.
We always listen to this at Christmas.
It's the first music I remember
from when I was very little.
Though the music is joyful,
we are
not.

Christmas is Christmas.
A fire burns in the fireplace.
Breakfast is sticky buns
and hot cocoa,
with mini-marshmallows melting on top.
There are presents for us.
We leave the presents for Strum
under the tree,
unopened.

I wish he could be here
to see the book I bought him
about the future
of climate science.

"Open your last present,"
Daddy tells me, handing me
a thin box.
It's a phone
and I grin and hug him
and then hug Maman.
"Thank you, thank you.
Finally!
I have to
call Strum."

Too late, I remember
and bite my lip. My throat
burns. Why did I say that?
I close my eyes,
wishing I could unsay the words.

Maman starts crying,
huge, messy sobs.
I open my eyes to see
Daddy take her in his arms,
rub her back in
gentle circles.

Aria gets up and
walks out of the room

and I realize
Christmas
is no longer my favorite
holiday.

Different Rooms

Throughout winter break,
the house is quiet,
too quiet,
with each of us
in a different room.
Why does it make me so unsettled?

When I'm not practicing
the oboe,
I'm reading.
That's quiet.
But also normal.

Daddy is doing
paperwork.
Silently.

Aria listens to music
with her earbuds
and draws a lot.
She's quiet.

If Strum were here,
he would probably be
on his laptop
in the slope-ceilinged room
over the garage.
He would have been
quiet too.
But all of that is normal.
And then I remember
what's wrong.

Maman never sings
anymore.

Part Three

Part Three

STACCATO

The Wolf's Identity

January is a *staccato*,
disconnected and
feeling detached.

In orchestra
we're now meeting three times a week
to practice
Peter and the Wolf
for the winter concert
we'll perform
in February,
whether Strum has been found
or not.

As I hold my oboe upright on my leg
and listen to the strings
play Peter's theme,
my heart catches,
thumps double time.

If Strum is Peter,
skipping through the dark forest,
then
who is
the wolf?

I Am a Walking Fraction

Without Strum, I've become a walking fraction,
although I go about my day as if I'm whole.

If my family is a pie cut in slices,
each of us makes one-fifth of the pie.

Without Strum, we're four-fifths of a circle.
Without Strum, I'm one-fourth of four-fifths.

And every time I calculate the answer,
One-fourth of four-fifths is one-fifth.

That's why math works. Because it never changes.

But I am still a fraction of myself.

The Color Blue

Over the weekend
I spend a lot of time
watching videos of Strum
on Daddy's laptop
in the den.
I haven't forgotten
what Strum looks like,
but I worry that I'll forget
what he *sounds* like.

Seventeen-year-old Strum
clowns around at Walden Pond
posing next to
the statue of Thoreau,
with his hand out,
contemplating nature.
"Look at me!" he cries.
"I'm contemplating nature!"

His sky-blue eyes sparkle.
But his voice is deep and sarcastic.
Strum! I want to scream.
I'm so mad at you!
French horns thunder
their forbidding music
inside my head.

Before I can continue, I have to
rearrange Daddy's desk.
Music composition books alphabetical
by the author. Spines perfectly even.
Pencils here, pens there, paper clips
in a container.
But I can't keep away from the screen
for long.

Fifteen-year-old Strum
tries to paddleboard
in St. Martin
while waves keep knocking
him off.
No matter how many times

he splashes into the water,
he keeps getting back up.

He hoots, shakes his wet head,
drops spraying out in a rainbow arc.
"Next time! I'll get it next time!"
The voice is confident, not quite as deep.
Strum!
I have to blink to see the screen.

Thirteen-year-old Strum
is building a birdhouse
at home.
"Hey, Dad."
Strum smiles at the camera.
"This is for bluebirds.
I'm thinking of
painting it bright blue with a red roof."

His voice is higher,
cheerful and strong. *Strum!*
Listening now,
my insides fill with blue.
Everywhere blue.
It's been a while
since Strum sounded
that happy.
It's been a while
since Strum built birdhouses,
but
he always loved
the color blue.

I go to bed,
with the nagging feeling
that my brain is trying
to tell me something.

Anything with Blue in It

During my next music lesson,
I'm still thinking about
the color blue.
And Strum.

Always Strum.

"Madrigal," Mr. Rimondi says.
"I think it's time to learn
something new."

I sit up straighter.
Something *new*?
It's been a while.
"Do you have anything
with the color blue in it?"

He smiles and nods,
riffles through stacks and stacks
of sheet music.
Finally,
he finds what he's
looking for,

handling it
by the page corners
as if it's rare and valuable.
"Ever heard of *Rhapsody in Blue*
by George Gershwin?"

I run my eyes over the music,
counting the beats.
"It's hard," he warns me.
"Lots of sharps and flats.
And it's fast. But you could
learn this."
My pulse speeds up to *allegro*.

Maybe
I could.
After all, Strum said,
Music is your superpower.

Something to Do

On Saturday,
after I finish my homework,
I come downstairs and realize
Maman is in the den.
She wears her reading glasses
and is bent over something
spread out on her lap.
Needlework.

She hasn't done any sewing
in years.
Not since the musical note throw pillows
for the living room sofa.

"What are you making?"
I ask.

She looks up,
her face blank,
as if she doesn't
remember
who I am.
What's wrong with her?
I'm not the one who's missing
but
I still *need* her,
need her
to
see
me.

"Oh," she says,
hand pressed to her chest.
"Maddie. You startled me."

She gestures at the hoop and
fabric in her lap.
"I just need...I needed
something to do
with my hands."

Maman needs something too.
I hadn't thought of that.
"Is it another pillow?"

She nods, shows me the photo on
the package.

A guitar
surrounded by lush
flowers in a rich deep blue.

Strum's favorite color.

A Decision

On Wednesday afternoon
I make a decision.
During free period,
instead of reading
in the back corner of the library,
I pack up my books
and go to Eco Club.

Emma's eyes widen
and her smile grows as big
as a symphony orchestra.
"You came!"
Oliver
didn't.

Emma introduces me to
Ms. Vidal,
the eighth-grade science teacher
and Eco Club moderator.
She's a round woman
with short black hair.
"Welcome, Maddie,"
says Ms. Vidal,
and her smile radiates
from her voice too.
"We're glad you're here."
The corners of my mouth
want to smile back.

"Do you know Bethann Myers
and Danny Fernandez?"
Emma asks. "They're in eighth grade."

"Not really," I mumble.
There are only three kids
in Eco Club? That's it?
No wonder Emma
begged me to join.

But I hate meeting new kids.
For one thing, I never know
what to say.
My mouth goes dry,
my tongue swells up.

I try to focus.
Try to really see these kids.

If I am classical music
and Emma with her zebra socks
is jazz,
then Bethann Myers is folk rock.
She's short
and wears a long swishy skirt and boots.
Her hair is frizzy
and, behind her glasses, her eyes are gray.
Bethann nods at me but doesn't smile.

Danny Fernandez is definitely hip-hop.
He wears an oversize green T-shirt and jeans
and has black hair, dark brown eyes.
Danny salutes me with a wide grin,
braces flashing.

Being Good Neighbors

"You've come at a great time,"
Ms. Vidal says to me.
"We're being
good neighbors today."
Apparently,
this means putting on
our coats
and bright orange vests.
Then we're supposed to go
outside to pick up trash
along Union Street.

Danny bounces on the balls of his feet,
like he can't wait to get out there.

Bethann protests,
"Why can't we just stay inside
and watch a video?
It's cold out there."

"You'll warm up
soon enough," Ms. Vidal says.
She winks at me,
hands out sturdy bags.
Makes sure we have gloves.

We walk along the edge of the school lawn,
picking up candy wrappers,
takeout containers,
squashed paper cups.

Emma holds up a plastic bottle.
"You'd think people
would know by now to recycle.
Or, better yet, buy a reusable water bottle
like we all have."

Strum always drank water
from a stainless steel bottle.
But Daddy and Maman buy
plastic water bottles for us.
I gulp. I need to ask Maman
to buy me a reusable bottle.

Emma picks up a crumpled
brown paper fast-food bag,
flattens it out.
"You could even reuse some of this stuff.
It could be drawing paper for little kids."

"That's a good idea," I say.

She nods and moves ahead.

Danny steps up next to me.
"So you're a musician like Emma?
That's cool. I like music.
Any kind of music. Mainly rap.
But also rock, punk, emo…"
Words pour out of him the way music
pours out of Oliver's oboe.
I try to hide my smile.

Danny reaches for a soda cup lid.
"I want to be an inventor.
Invent stuff like solar cars,
solar power tools."
He grins at me,
braces winking.

Even though Eco Club
isn't quite what I thought
it would be,
I'm glad I came.

Being outside,
and actually doing something,

makes me feel
less helpless.

And, besides, Danny's kind of cute.

Something More Important

"Thanks for joining,"
Emma says as we wait in the bus line
after school.

"It was fun," I say.
"I didn't realize that's the kind
of stuff you do."

She shifts her backpack.
"Oh, it's different every week.
You know, sometimes we watch videos,
sometimes we make posters."

I nod.

"I wish," she says,
brushing her bangs
out of her face. "I wish
we could do something
more important.
Most grown-ups don't seem
to care enough.
Someone has to be responsible

for this planet.
It's the only one we have."

This is true but
it makes me feel
hopeless.

A Test

After geometry on Friday
Nico says, "Want to study
for the test together
this weekend?"

I head for the door.
"You want to study with *me*?"

He shrugs. "Why not? We can quiz
each other. I could come over
after dinner tomorrow."
He waggles his dark eyebrows.
"I know where you live."

He's so funny and warm
I can't help grinning back.
"Oh, you just want to see *Aria*."

He ducks his head
so I can't see his face.
I giggle.

"I do like your sister,"
he says softly.

"No! *Really?*"
Joking with Nico
feels normal. I'm so ready
for normal.

The tips of Nico's ears turn red.
"Tell you what," he says.
"I'll come at six instead and
bring pizza."

This makes me smile.
"Bring two." *A better number.*
"With extra cheese."
He grins.

Extra Cheese

When Nico shows up
on Saturday,
Maman answers the door.
Coming up behind her,
I inhale the warm cardboard smell
of pizza boxes.
Maman's still holding the doorknob,
her face shadowed with confusion.
"May I help you?"

I duck under her arm.
"Remember, Maman?
I told you Nico was bringing pizza."
She closes her eyes and shakes her head.

Nico smiles.
"Hey, thanks," I say.
"Did you remember extra cheese?"

"Rats!" His face falls.
He trudges past us
into the kitchen
and sets down the boxes
as if they're *terribly* heavy.
When I open the top box,
melting cheese
oozes everywhere.
"You *did* remember!"
He grins. I want to punch him
and hug him at the same time.

There are eight slices in a pizza.
Sixteen slices in two pizzas.
The most beautiful even numbers.

As Daddy hands out plates,
Aria appears, looking dazed.
"Nico? What are you doing here?
What's going on?"
Nico grins at her. "Hey, muchacha.
Pizza.
Pizza is going on."

Aria shakes her head but smiles.
She doesn't seem to mind Nico
calling her girl.

We take seats
around the kitchen table.
The V-shaped worry lines
in Maman's forehead deepen.
In a flash, I understand.
Nico is sitting in Strum's seat.

I try not to think about it as I wolf
down my first slice, counting the bites,
willing my stomach to stay calm.

"Thank you, young man," Daddy says.

"His name is Nico," Aria says.

Nico murmurs something to Aria,
who says, "No way!
"You're studying with the Mad One?"

Nico winks at me. "In case you didn't know it,
she's buenísima at math."

The back of my neck grows warm.
Aria rolls her eyes, as if to say,
don't remind me.
But Maman gives me a fond look.
"Of course she's excellent!"
I'd forgotten she knows Spanish.
Daddy nods. "That's our girl."

As we eat, Nico entertains us
with impersonations of his teachers.
Aria and I share a rare grin
when he pinches his face into a frown
like Mrs. Turner.
Aria had her last year.

It's another hour before
we even open our math books.

Practice, Practice, Practice

Over the weekend,
I spend so much time
practicing *Rhapsody in Blue*
my lips swell up.

Then I switch to the solos
in *Peter and the Wolf.*
I practice and practice,
trying to
call
Strum
home.

But my mouth hurts so much
the notes come out as sour squeaks.

I think I need a break.

Polar Bears

The following week
in Eco Club,
we pledge to
take the thermostat challenge
and keep our homes
at 68 degrees Fahrenheit.
Brrr, I think.

"That's being kind
to the Earth," Emma says.
"We all need to reduce
our carbon footprint."

"No problem,"
Danny says. "I'm always warm
anyway."
It's January
and he's wearing
a T-shirt.

Bethann is wearing layers,
a dark shirt over a white turtleneck.
Emma and I wear sweaters,
although mine is nubby and
too short
in the sleeves now.

Then
we watch a video

of scientists in their parkas
in northern Canada,
talking about polar bears.
International Polar Bear Day
is coming up in late February.

"Maybe you can convince
your parents
to let you adopt a polar bear,"
Ms. Vidal says.

"For real?" Bethann asks.
Emma and Danny laugh.

Ms. Vidal smiles.
"Well, it's symbolic.
Your donation would help
real polar bears in the wild.
And fund research
on the effects of
climate change
on their habitats.
But they call it adopting."

I slide down in my seat.
Knowing my parents, they won't
agree.
But I'll bet Emma would love
to do that. Adopt a polar bear.

She frowns and looks down
at her desk.

Then I remember
she lives in a small house
with a tiny yard.
They never go on vacation.
Her mom doesn't seem to have
extra money.
What could I do?
I'll have to think about it.

Next, we watch a live feed
of polar bears
wandering across the tundra.

If Strum decided
to walk north
to see the polar bears,
wouldn't he be
too cold
in just a hoodie?
I shiver.

Ms. Vidal asks,
"Any ideas on how we could
celebrate Polar Bear Day?"

"Make posters!" Emma says.
"Let everyone know how important
the Arctic sea ice is.
If it keeps melting,
polar bears will lose their home."

Ms. Vidal nods. "Good idea."

Danny says, "Let's cancel classes
and go outside
and have a snowball fight!"

"Danny!" Emma and Bethann shout
in unison.

I can't help smiling
but have to point out the obvious.
"It hasn't even snowed yet."

A Winter Memory

Last winter,
Strum's senior year in high school,
we had a huge snowstorm.
Afterward, Daddy and Strum and I
went out to shovel the driveway.

Aria didn't want to help
but she pulled on boots and a jacket
and walked around
taking pictures of frosted branches
and curved mounds of
snowdrift.

We only have three shovels
anyway.
I used the smallest one.
As we cleared the heavy snow,

Daddy goaded Strum.
"Still insist on calling this
global warming?"

Strum made a growling sound
low in his throat and said,
"*Climate change*, Dad. It's climate change.
Actually, a climate *crisis*."

Aria, in the front yard,
whipped her head around,
her hair falling
across the lens of her camera.

Daddy snorted.
"Climate change. Of course.
Can't exactly call it global warming
if it's thirty-one degrees out here,
with a boatload of snow."
He rammed his shovel into a high drift.

Hearing Daddy and Strum
argue made me nervous.
To calm myself, I sucked in
slow deep breaths, counting
one   two   three   four,
between each shovelful of snow.

Strum tossed a load
of snow to one side.
"Dad, you're confusing weather
with climate.
This is exactly what

scientists have
warned us about.
Extreme conditions,
unusual weather patterns,
droughts,
superstorms.
And the Arctic sea ice is
melting,
pushing the cold air down to us.
It's all part of a growing crisis.
Our planet
is in deep trouble."

Daddy just laughed,
shook his head,
and kept
shoveling.

Defiance

On Thursday
in English class
Mr. Hartshorne looks at Emma
and frowns.
What is his problem?
Usually, Mr. Hartshorne is
one of my favorite teachers.
When he assigns an essay,
he says, "Neatness counts."
He's the only teacher

who wears a tie—and it's always straight.
He makes us line up our desks
with the green X's on the tile floor.

But today he says to Emma,
"School rules clearly state
no pins with sayings.
I'm afraid you'll have to
put that away, Miss Chen."
Emma covers her *Save Our Sea Ice*
pin with her palm.
"But—"
Mr. Hartshorne shakes his head.
"Don't try to justify it.
It's against the rules."

"No," Emma says.
My mouth falls open.
How brave!
There are scattered gasps and murmurs
from the rest of the class.
Emma really cares about the climate crisis.
She's a better person
than I am.
Right then I vow
to be a better friend to her.

Emma straightens her spine.
"The Arctic sea ice
is melting more rapidly than scientists thought.
I'm just trying
to raise awareness."

Mr. Hartshorne grows rigid and
speaks through clenched teeth. "The pin.
Take off the pin
so we can continue with this class."

Emma stands up.

Mr. Hartshorne's graying eyebrows arch.
"Young lady, where do you think
you're going?"
She walks out of the classroom,
beckoning us
to join her.

I didn't expect I'd have to fulfill my vow
immediately.
And I don't want to.
Everything needs
to be in its proper place.
Including me.

Swallowing down the sour taste
rising in my throat, I look around
at my classmates,
kids I rarely talk to,
and issue a silent challenge.
Then I stand up and follow Emma.

Three kids follow me,
Marisol, Jason,
and Topher.
(Topher? I nearly fall over in surprise.)

Three kids.
Not a good number.
But maybe
Emma and I just recruited three more
members of the Eco Club.

Mr. Hartshorne is yelling now,
"Come back here! I didn't dismiss you."
No way I'm going back.
I have to see what Emma
is doing.

Mr. Hartshorne storms
down the hallway behind us.
Silently, Emma raises her arm and points
to the words etched in stone
over the entryway to
Margaret Murie Middle School.
"You are only half a person
if you do not care."

Mr. Hartshorne splutters, "Get back
in the classroom this minute or you're all
getting detention."

Emma squares her shoulders.
"Margaret Murie helped protect
what is now
the Arctic National Wildlife Refuge.
Are you telling us we shouldn't
care, Mr. Hartshorne?"

Danny comes walking
down the hallway,
his jacket and backpack on.
"Are you leaving?" I ask in a whisper.

"Orthodontist," he whispers back,
grinning. "What's going on?"
I fill him in
as the principal comes out of her office.
Her heels click-clack on the tile floor.
Nine click-clacks. I wince.

The principal stops, stands straight,
looking at each of us in turn.

"Ms. Ying," Emma pipes up. "We need
to have a climate strike
like other schools have had.
Older generations
are ignoring the crisis."

Emma falters when Ms. Ying frowns at her.
"Or at least, um, maybe an *assembly* about the
climate crisis..."

"An assembly would be fine, Emma. But
you need to ask your club moderator to
apply for it."

The principal turns to our teacher.
"Mr. Hartshorne? Care to explain?"

He clears his throat.
"Everything's under control, Ms. Ying.
These five students
have detention with me
tomorrow afternoon."

But tomorrow's Friday.
I'll miss my music lesson.

Detention

I've never had
detention before.
You can't talk in detention,
which would be okay because
I don't talk much anyway.
But my stomach wants to leave.

So I count.

I count the tiles on the floor,
the stains in the ceiling,
the books on a shelf,
hoping they'll come out even.
None of them do.
Emma smiles at me
and I try to smile back.

I am missing my music lesson
for this.

Maman made me call
Mr. Rimondi myself last night.
He was disappointed and warned me
to keep practicing.

The other three kids,
Topher, Jason, and Marisol,
look as sick as I feel.

Mr. Hartshorne gets a big
surprise when Danny
and Bethann show up too.
"Hi!" Danny says, braces flashing.
"We're here to
serve a detention in solidarity
with Emma. We support her stand!"
Bethann nods
but she doesn't look happy.
Danny must have
talked her into it.
Mr. Hartshorne sighs and says,
"Have a seat."

Inside me, a laugh wants to bubble up.
Now I don't feel so sick.
Bethann looks a little shaky, though.
Danny just sits there, grinning.
Maybe he's thinking of
a good joke or
dreaming up a new
solar invention.
Emma glances at each of us

and her eyes are saying
"Thank you."

Friends don't need words
to talk.

Daddy's Voice

Dinner starts out quietly until...
     Daddy sets down his glass with a thump.
"Detention? Maddie, what were you
thinking?"

"Chéri." Maman tries to hush him.
I know by the droop of her shoulders
that she's disappointed in me.
But her set face says
it's already happened. It's
over.

From the growl
in Daddy's voice, though,
I know he's furious.
Furious voice is worse
than stern voice.
Furious voice is the one
he used on Strum a lot last year.
It makes my cheeks burn.
A muscle in Daddy's jaw
tightens.
His breathing roughens.

Now

Now I hear what Strum heard.
Now I see what Strum saw.
Now I feel what Strum felt.

Aria Speaks

Aria has been silent
until now. She says,
"You did the right thing, Mad.
Standing up for your friend like that."
I'm so shocked I drop my fork
and have to scramble under the table
to reach it.
Maman gets me a new fork
without a word.

I look at Aria.
"You think what I did was *right*?"

Aria looks at me, really looks at me,
for the first time in a while.
"Yeah. Someone has to take responsibility
for this planet. Might as well
be our generation. Since the older one
screwed it up so bad."

I nod. "That's what Emma says."

Maman frowns.
Daddy shakes his head,
narrows his eyes,
but pinches his lips together,
not rising
to Aria's bait.

Aria and I smile at each other.
A sister grin.

Being a Sister

After dinner,
I load the dishwasher.
Maman and Daddy put leftover food away.
Aria announces she's going out.

Maman rubs her forehead.
"With whom? And where?"

Daddy says, "Just a minute, young lady!
Do I know this guy?
Is it Nico, the one who brought the pizzas?"

Aria walks out of the kitchen.
"I didn't say
it was a guy. Just *out*.
With *friends*.
They're picking me up."

I look from Maman to Daddy,
counting the worry lines.
Before, I would have stayed out of this,
would have delighted in the look
on Daddy's face if it meant
Aria was in trouble.
Now I mumble,
"You let Strum go out when
he was sixteen.
And Aria's almost seventeen!"

Mumbling is totally against the rules.
So is being a smart mouth.
Aria is a master at both but
I've always followed the rules.

Tonight, I'm not following the rules.

Daddy starts to say something

but stops himself, jaw muscles twitching.

Maman turns to look at me,
her eyes wide, glistening.
"What did you say?"

What?
Are we not supposed to *mention*
Strum anymore?
He's not dead!
I refuse to believe that.

Calling Nico

When I finish the dishes
I go up to my room and
call Nico.
"Maddie, what's up?"

"Aria said she's going out with *friends*.
Is she meeting you?"

Nico swears softly.
"No, she didn't mention anything.
But I'm pretty sure I know where
she's going.
Remember those other kids
who were at your house that night?
The ones who brought the beer?"

I picture that night and cringe.
Start counting the books on my shelf.
Onetwothreefourfivesixseveneight.

"Maddie?"

"Yeah, I remember."

"I'll go see them.
Don't worry. I'll find her.
And I won't let her do anything stupid.
I promise."

"Thanks, Nico. Just…thanks."

"Anytime, muchachita."

I don't think I mind being called
little girl anymore by Nico.
Muchachita is such a cheerful-sounding word.

Butterfly Dreams

That night
I dream I am
a butterfly.
A blue morpho,
flying free,
appearing and disappearing
among green leaves.
The dream fades into blue
and green wisps,
leaving me with the odd feeling
that something is
just out of
my reach.
It's a nice dream,
a soothing dream,
and then I wake up,
knowing Strum is still

missing.

Part Four

CRESCENDO

Bolero

February is
a *crescendo,*
gradually growing
brighter
and more exuberant.
Like *Bolero,*
a one-movement orchestral piece
by Maurice Ravel.

Halfway through *Bolero*
the French horns and
bell-like celesta
enter and the music
grows livelier.

These French horns don't threaten.
These French horns play notes that rise and swell.
These French horns lift me up.

I listen to *Bolero* and think about
my family.
Try to make sense
of things.

Aria
shuts herself in her room
and barely talks to us.

Maman
wanders through the house,
looking as if
she's forgotten something
in another room.

Daddy
stares at the TV for hours,
a vacant look in his eyes.

Strum isn't dead.
I refuse to believe that.

But they're acting more and more
like *they* are.

Never Is a Frightening Word

"They're never going to
find him,"
Aria says one night
at dinner.
Trust Aria to say
out loud
what we've all been
thinking.

I don't realize Maman
is crying
until I see the tears
glistening

on her cheeks,
dripping off
her chin.
She cries silently,
shoulders quaking.
Daddy's eyes narrow
and his Adam's apple
bobs in his throat.

I'm jumpy, anxious.
Can't handle seeing
Maman's tears.
To calm down,
I count the silverware
on the table,
nineteneleventwelve.

What will happen
if they never find Strum?
Will our family be in limbo
forever?
What can I do?
My family is grieving.
Suffering.
Lost.

All of us.

Letting the Music Help

Mr. Rimondi said, *Let the music help.*

Strum said,
Music is your superpower.

Music is what I do best.

Maybe I can play my oboe
for my family.
Maybe if they hear bright music
they'll feel better.

So I bring my oboe
downstairs
and sit at the piano with
my sheet music.
The jazzy, quicksilver notes of
Rhapsody in Blue
draw them out,
one by one.

Maman comes in first,
taking a seat on the couch.
Daddy walks in,
hands in his pockets.

After a moment,
Aria joins them.

"Thank God," she says,
"it's not the duck
anymore."

"Nonsense," Maman says,
her eyes still red.
"Everything Maddie plays is
lovely."
She smiles a watery smile.
Daddy nods in time to the tempo.
Aria looks at the ceiling.

"Merci beaucoup, Maddie,"
Maman says when I finish.
Thank you very much.
"That was lovely.
Hunter, you could
accompany her on the piano.
Play a duet."

So Daddy and I play "Ode to Joy"
from *Symphony No. 9*
by Ludwig van Beethoven.
It's the brightest, most jubilant music
I know.

It's also a Catholic hymn we call
"Joyful, Joyful, We Adore Thee."

For the first time in months,
Maman hums. The humming
grows louder and
brighter and
finally blooms into
a song.

It's a start.

Aria and I share
a look, a nod.

Then Aria Ruins the Mood

Daddy stands up,
points at the piano bench.
"Aria, play something
for us."

Aria scowls,
ruining the mood.
"Don't be ridiculous, Dad.
I haven't played in years,
not since you
forced lessons on us."

Daddy frowns.
"I *forced* lessons on you?"

In our family,
piano lessons with Daddy
were the rule,
starting at age eight.

When Strum's lessons started,
I was only a baby,
so I don't remember.

When Aria's lessons started,
I was four.

I remember prancing around
the living room while Aria
slumped at the piano next to Daddy
and banged on the keys.
It seemed like fun to me.
But she wasn't smiling.

Now Aria says to Daddy,
"You forced Strum to learn.
I was five. I remember
him saying, 'I don't want to do this!
You can't make me!'
It scared me so much
I *dreaded* turning eight."

Daddy's face whitens,
his blue eyes turn frosty.
He starts to open his mouth
but
Maman says, "Ça suffit!"
That's enough!

Aria flounces out of the room.

I stare at the piano.
Is that why I never play anymore?
Is that why I took up the oboe instead?

Something Positive

On Wednesday,
Eco Club
gets to go on a field trip
and miss most of our classes.
Emma and I are happy
to miss English class.
So is Topher, who has
joined the club too.
Why did it have to be
Topher?
The world's worst
smirker?
Why not Jason or Marisol?

I try to think of something positive.
Danny seems happy
that Topher's there. They're
clowning around,
punching each other in the
shoulder.
Guys.

Emma and Bethann and I
look at each other
and shake our heads
at the same time.
This makes me smile.

Before we get on the bus,
Emma says, "Ms. Vidal,

could we have
an assembly about the climate crisis?
Sometime soon?"

I was hoping she'd forgotten
about her conversation with the principal.

"We need to get across to *everyone*
how urgent this is.
Our world is melting.
Coastal areas are flooding.
Animals are losing their habitats."

Ms. Vidal holds up both hands.
"Whoa. Emma, you don't have
to convince me. I agree!
And that would be fine.
Let's work out a plan
at the next Eco Club."

Emma nods. "Thank you."

The Field Trip

The field trip takes us
all the way to
the Franklin Institute,
one of my favorite places
in the whole world.
We are here to see a special
exhibit about climate change.

But there's time to explore
the entire institute.
We even bring bagged lunches
and eat in their cafeteria.
Bethann watches me arrange
my sandwich quarters
a thumb-width apart
before eating them.
"Why do you do that?" she asks,
squinting behind her glasses.

I shrug. "I just like to, that's all."

Emma looks as if
she swallowed a lemon.
"Have you forgotten?" she says to Bethann.
"Maddie's stressed because her brother's
missing."

It's nice of her to defend me
but I can defend myself.
I think.

And then I gasp.
Arranging my sandwich quarters
is something I did
before Strum disappeared.
Months before.
Maybe even a year.
Like counting.

I count the tables in the cafeteria.
Eightnineteneleventwelve.

Across the table,
Bethann makes a *humph* sound.
"Sorry.
But I get stressed too.
When my parents talk to me
about my weight, all I want to do is
eat more."

I swallow and look at Bethann.
"It's okay," I say with a boldness
that comes from I-don't-know-where,
"you just haven't had
your growth spurt yet."

Everyone laughs and laughs,
but it's a good kind of laughing
and Bethann looks at me,
her face open in surprise.
But at least she smiles.

Topher looks at me too,
eyes narrowed,
as if he's thinking hard,
trying to see inside my head.

Harriet the Spy

Topher says,
"I've watched you at school.
You always eat the same lunch."

My heart races. So he noticed that
while he smirked at me.
I take a bite of
my turkey sandwich.

"Leave her alone,"
Danny says, his voice a snarl.

But Topher leans toward me,
his thin brown hair
falling in his eyes.
"No, it's cool. I mean, you're just like
Harriet the Spy.
She always ate a tomato sandwich.
Every single day.
Remember?"

Emma tilts her head.
"That's right, Topher. I loved that book!"
I smile, despite myself. "So did I."

"If I could,"
Danny says,
"I'd eat cheeseburgers every day."

Topher grins. "Sweet potato fries."
My heart skips a beat.
Strum's favorite food.

Emma nods. "Radishes."
We all look at her.
"What?" she says,

lifting her hands.
"I like radishes."

Bethann laughs. "Not me. I'd have
a hot fudge sundae
with tons of whipped cream

every

single

day."

And we bubble over with laughter.

But then Ms. Vidal
tells us to finish up so we can
go see the exhibit.
She reminds us that's why
we're here.

I clean up every crumb
and put my trash
in the bin.
Everything in its place.
As we walk away,
laughing and talking
about food,
I feel for the first time
that I'm really part of
a group.

Even with Topher.

Appear and Disappear

In the rainforest part
of the climate change exhibit
a blue butterfly catches my eye.

I grab Emma's arm.
"What?" she says. "Did you find
something cool?"
Danny stands on my other side,
looking from me to the display.
"What is it?" he asks.

Shiny blue wings
edged in speckled black.
Could it be?
A blue morpho?
I hold myself together,
trying not to squeal.
"Blue morpho!"
I take four deep breaths.

The label says *Morpho peleides* butterflies
live in Central America
and southeastern Mexico,
flourishing in the rainforest.
And they don't migrate
like monarchs do.

But with the destruction
of the rainforest,
blue morphos are losing

their habitat.
I remember the blue morphos
at the Butterfly Farm
and how they seemed to
appear and disappear.

Flying

Blue morphos flying,
appear and then disappear.
Nature's magicians.

Everything in Its Place

As I stare at the display,
something clicks in my brain.

Everything

    in

       its

         place.

Sometimes all you need to do
is keep quiet
and listen.

And you will hear deep inside yourself
the tiny whisper of truth.

I can't believe I didn't
see it before.

Distracted by polar bears,
I forgot every living thing
is connected.
Forgot other species
are threatened too.
Forgot every country
is affected by this crisis.

Strum's emails mentioned

     climate change

     Frida Kahlo

     St. Martin

My mind sings
as clear and strong
as a sustained middle C.
Because I get it now.
What he was hinting.
I know
where Strum is.

I
know

where
Strum
is.

Google Always Tells You

I remember how Strum reacted
to the framed
dead blue morphos
in the gift shop.

That's the answer.
That's when he started caring
about the climate crisis.

I grab my phone. Feverishly,
my thumbs flying
over the virtual keyboard,
I search Google.

Google tells me
blue morphos
can be found in
the Lacandon Jungle
of Mexico,
near the border with Guatemala.
Much of that rainforest
has been destroyed
by lumbering
and cattle ranching.

But a large section
has been preserved.
Montes Azules Biosphere Reserve.
Within that reserve is a lake
called Laguna Miramar.

I roll the words around on my tongue,
loving the sound,
smooth as river stones.
Laguna Miramar.

From Fort Collins, Colorado,
to Laguna Miramar
is a long way to walk.
Google says the driving time
is 43 hours.
But it would take
approximately
783 hours to walk.
Even if Strum could walk
for 8 hours a day
it would take him at least 97 days.

Strum could do it.
I know he could.
He might even
ride a bus or
hitchhike part of the way.
Strum would want
to see the blue morphos
before the rainforest

disappears.
Before deforestation
ruins
their habitat.
Before the world
as we know it
changes.

All blue morphos want to do
is fly free.

French horns bellow inside my head.
Strum! I scream silently,
Strum!
What are you doing?
What were you thinking?
Why didn't you say *anything?*

When I Tell Maman and Daddy

At dinner,
when I tell Maman and Daddy
my new theory,
Daddy looks away,
frowning.
I can tell he doesn't believe me.
Neither does Aria, who
shakes her head
as if I'm making up
fairy tales.

But Maman stands up,
wipes away tears, and
goes to call Detective Sanderson.
"I know it's not likely,"
Maman says into the phone.
"But can you at least consider it?
S'il vous plaît? Please?"

Now we wait.

Days Go By

There is no word.
There is no update.
There is no change.

If No One Else Is Going, I Will

Even though it's February
and it's 30 degrees Fahrenheit outside
(or minus 1 Celsius)
someone needs to look for Strum.
If no one else is going,

I will.

Google tells me it's a long way from
Bennett Corners to Laguna Miramar.

Nearly 2950 miles.
I can't walk that far.
The closest bus station is in
Wilmington, Delaware.

Wilmington to San Antonio
looks like the most direct route.
From San Antonio, I'll have to walk to Mexico.

There's a bus at eight o'clock tonight.
It's three o'clock now. If I leave right away,
I could get to the station before dark.

The bus will cost me
all the birthday and Christmas money
I have saved.

The station is thirteen miles away.
Thirteen miles? I can walk that.
It's not an even number, and that
makes me shudder,
but I know
I can do it.

Weighing Me Down

I fill a backpack with ten protein bars,
six water bottles, and my phone,
put on leggings
under jeans,

pull on my heaviest sweater
and my thick winter coat.
A hat and gloves.

I take my money
from the secret stash under my bed.
Now I'm ready.

The backpack weighs me down,
as I march south on Creek Road
toward Delaware
for twenty minutes,
the cold breeze stinging my eyes.
My breath puffs out
in fist-size clouds.

Then I begin
to falter.

Maman and Daddy
will be upset when they realize
I'm gone.
Even Aria might miss me.

That's when it hits me
like a punch in the stomach
that I would miss
Aria
if she disappeared.
Maybe almost as much
as I miss Strum.

I step off the frosted grass
to cross a side street
and a car honks at me,
making me jump back.

Is this the right thing to do?
My pace slows even more.
Maybe I'm not brave enough.

Backpack

I didn't like when Aria left me
for the evening
to go out with friends.
I didn't like when Maman
and Daddy left.
And Strum's leaving ruined
everything.

If I leave home now,
then not only is Strum out of place,
I will be too.

Everything needs to be
in its place.

Maybe I *can't* find Strum
on my own.
But I can get myself home.

Back at the house,
I let myself in,
peel off the layers
as I start to sweat.
Gizmo dozes in a patch
of afternoon sunlight. I let him sleep.

I go up to my room
and practice
the duck solos
from *Peter and the Wolf,*
just like every day,
counting the beats
onetwothreefour,
and trying to pretend
nothing happened.

Daddy and Maman,
watching TV in their room,
didn't even notice
I was gone.

Aria taps on my open door.
She squints at me,
her face
caving in on itself.
"Where *were* you?"

I grip my oboe,
keep my voice *pianissimo.*
"Um, I went for a walk."

She looks at my open backpack,
bottles of water
and protein bars
poking out.
"Did you…?
Oh, Mad.
Were you planning to *walk*
to Mexico?"

My throat stings from
held-back tears.
I shake my head.
"The bus station."

"Come here."
She folds me into a hug.
That's when I start blubbering.
I sob and shudder and cough.
It's the first time I've really cried
over Strum.
As my sobbing quiets down
another sound rises.
Aria crying too.

Butterflies in the Air

Friday,
at my music lesson,
the sunlight outside
Mr. Rimondi's window
fills me up, makes me feel

as if I'm floating.
It's lighter later now.
I might even have a chance to swing
or take Gizmo for a walk
in the woods
before dinner.

Mr. Rimondi asks me to play
the oboe solo parts
in *Peter and the Wolf.*
"But I'm second oboe,"
I say. "I don't have a solo."

Mr. Rimondi smiles. "Play it
anyway."
He taps his forehead.
"I know
you've been practicing
at home."

How does he know that?
Adults are like a foreign country.
I look at the sheet music,
take two deep calming breaths
and think of Strum
chasing butterflies.
Think of Maman singing,
Aria drawing,
Daddy playing the piano.

And I begin.

I play
how much I miss Strum
and his bright laughter.
I play the sadness
of Emma's polar bears.
I play the melting Arctic sea ice.

Maybe I am not
a metronome
after all.
Maybe I *do*
have feelings.
Maybe I *can* be
good enough.

"Madrigal," Mr. Rimondi says
when I finish.
"That was incredible."
His hands are butterflies
in the air.

Inside the Stomach of the Wolf

Mr. Dahlberg must have noticed
I've been working hard.
At the end of our next rehearsal,
he tells me I will play
the first solo.
It's not the one I want to play,
the solo where the duck quacks

mournfully from inside
the stomach of the wolf.
Instead, it's the earlier one
where the duck decides to go
for a swim in the pond.
Same theme, different tempo.

"But if you can't handle it,"
Mr. Dahlberg says,
pointing a bony finger
at me, "Oliver will step in."

I nod. "That—that's fine. Thank you!"
Then I try to smile at Oliver,
but he won't look my way.
"It's just one solo," I whisper.
"You're still the first
oboist."

He pushes his perfect hair
back from his forehead,
making it stick up in odd places,
and shrugs.
"It's only the
student version
of *Peter and the Wolf.*
It's not hard.
But who knows?
You're getting
pretty good."

Then he gives me
a quick grin.

It appears and disappears
so fast
I wonder if I
imagined it.

I Have a Solo

I have a solo now. My heart feels light.
Maybe this means that Strum will come back home.
In case it does, I'll practice every night.

Ideas, Anyone?

At Eco Club,
Emma raises her hand.
"Ms. Vidal, you said we could
talk about a climate change assembly."

Ms. Vidal nods.

"I think *we* should present it.
Us five."

Topher groans and even Bethann rolls her eyes.
Danny sits up straighter, though.

Will we have to run
this assembly *ourselves*?

In front of the whole school?
My mouth goes dry.

Ms. Vidal writes "Assembly" on the SMART Board,
then turns back to us.
"Ideas, anyone?"

Emma can barely sit still.
"Let's show that video
from the polar bear organization!"

Danny nods. "Good idea!"

Ms. Vidal writes "Polar Bear Video" on the board.

Danny says,
"We should give kids suggestions
for what they can do at home.
Recycling, buying reusable grocery bags,
convincing their parents to
get solar panels if they can afford it."

Emma bounces up and down.
"Yes! Great idea! And they should ask
their parents to drive electric cars."

Ms. Vidal writes "What kids can do"
on the board.

Emma nearly leaps out of her seat.
It's the most animated I've ever seen her.
It makes me smile.
She's really into this.

"We could show before-and-after
photos of places like
the Great Barrier Reef in Australia.
To show the bleaching out, you know?
And the glaciers in Antarctica that are thinning.
Oh, and we should definitely show them
photos of
the Great Pacific Garbage Patch!"

Writing on the board,
Ms. Vidal laughs. "Slow down, Emma!"

But Emma plows on.
"I know! Let's have a Q&A session!
Have kids ask climate questions.
And *we* answer them."

My shoulders sag.
Answer questions? Out loud?
In front of the whole school?
I'm learning,
but I don't know that much about
climate change yet.

Topher looks at me,
his face twisted in agony.
He doesn't want
to do this either!

I'm just about to open my mouth
to say I don't want to answer
students' questions,
when Bethann raises her hand.

"I vote Emma gives the answers."
She looks at Emma. "You're
the expert.
And maybe Danny wants to help.
But *I'm* not answering questions on the spot.
I'll help you find photos and stuff."

Warmth floods my face.
Thank you, Bethann.
Topher lets out his breath in a whoosh.
I give him a little smile.

"I can do that," Emma says.
"How about next week?"

Ms. Vidal laughs, her stomach wiggling.
"Oh, this won't happen until
March or April at the earliest."

Emma twists her mouth,
slides down in her seat.

Then she pops back up again.
"Hey, I know! Let's have it on
Earth Day!"

Outnumbered

That night,
I'm reading in my room,

rain thrumming against my windows,
when loud voices erupt
downstairs.
It's a good book
and I don't want to leave it
but
something is wrong.

"Not this late
on a school night!"
Daddy shouts.
"Absolument pas,
young lady!" Maman yells.
Absolutely not.
"What about homework?"

If Daddy is
thundering bass drums,
Maman is a downpour
of cymbals.
I can't remember
the last time
Maman raised her voice.

Outside, a car horn honks.
Aria screams, "I don't care
what you think!"
The front door slams
before I'm halfway down
the stairs.
I stop, gripping the banister.

Maman looks up at me,
her face stony.
"Do you have any idea
where your sister
is going?"
I squint. "Isn't she with Nico?"
Maman shakes her head.
Daddy storms into the den.

I run back up to the safety
of my room and call Nico.
"Aria's gone again.
Can you find her?
Bring her home?"

"It's raining, muchachita."

"Please, Nico?"

He sighs.
"I'll see what I can do."

An hour later
Nico brings Aria back,
the cold smell of rain blowing in with them.
I ease down to my halfway spot
on the stairs, crouching.
From here I can see the foyer
and most of the living room.
But I'm not sure I want to be
in the middle of this,

to witness
Aria's cloud of anger,
Daddy's thunder,
Maman's downpour of sobs.

Aria peels off
her damp coat,
leaving it in a heap
on the floor.
Maman and Daddy
don't even notice,
but it makes me shudder
and clench my fists.

She flings herself on the sofa
in the living room,
crossing her arms.

My parents are standing in the foyer
with Nico.
"Thank you, Nico,"
Maman says faintly,
polite in spite of everything.

Raindrops glisten on Nico's hair.
"Uh, you're welcome.
But Mrs. Lovato, Mr. Lovato,
Aria isn't exactly
happy with me.
I can't keep doing this."
He wipes his hair back,
looks at his shoes.

Maman's shoulders sag.
Daddy shifts his weight
from one foot to the other.

Safe in my hiding spot,
I hug my knees,
count
the shoelace holes in my sneakers,
teneleventwelve,
and wish
Strum were here.

Everything fell apart
when Strum disappeared.

Nico shuffles his feet.
"I know it's not really
my place to say this, but
I told Aria
she needs counseling.
I—I think you all do."
Counseling.
The meaning of the word startles me
but the sound is
soothing,
almost musical. A waltz.
Counseling. COUN se ling

Daddy steps forward,
shakes a finger in Nico's face.
"Now you listen to me, young man.

This is none of your business.
We're handling this.
And we don't need anyone's help."

From my place
in the shadows,
I cringe.
"We're grateful you brought
Aria home," Daddy adds,
"but you may leave now."
I'm rocking back and forth,
wishing I were brave.
And then I think—

Wait.

I *could* be brave.
Fear floods through me
but I won't let it
control me anymore.

I can't hide any longer.
I clomp down the rest
of the steps,
watch their heads turn.
Take a deep breath.
"It was *my* idea.
I called Nico. *I* asked him
to bring her back."

Aria stands up,
flings her arms wide.

"Why would you do that?
I just wanted to have a little fun.
This house is so
de*pressing*."

My voice sinks to a whisper.
"Aria, I don't want *you*
disappearing
too."
She bites her lip, her eyes wide
and glistening.

I wrap my arms around myself
to keep from shaking.
And a quiet voice inside me
whispers,
Counseling. You can talk to someone.
About the throw-up feeling. The counting.
I turn to my parents.
"Nico's right.
We need counseling.
All of us."

Maman nods slowly.
"C'est vrai." *It's true.*
She reaches out and hugs Aria,
who says, "Okay, okay. Fine."

Then Maman hugs me.
I squeeze her hard.
Breathe in her calming lavender scent.

Nico's eyes widen,
as if he's afraid she'll hug him too.
"I should get going," he says.

After Nico leaves,
Daddy's chest sags.
The fight
has gone out of him.
His mouth droops
as if he just now
realizes
he's been

outnumbered.

Butterflies in My Stomach

At our next rehearsal,
I miss the A-flat
and flub the first few notes
of my solo.

Mr. Dahlberg taps his baton
on his music stand.
"Okay, okay. Let's try that
again."
He gives me a stern look,
making me think,
I'm not good enough.
I press my lips together,

not even wanting
to try.
Count the lines in the sheet music.
Sixseveneightnineten.
Mr. Dahlberg raises his baton.

"You can do this,
Maddie,"
Oliver whispers.
"I've heard you."
I glance at him,
my eyebrows asking questions.
He nods.
Gives me a thumbs-up.

Butterflies appear and disappear
in my stomach.
I let out my breath.
Then I carefully adjust
my fingering
and try again.

This time it's right.
But my heart is waltzing
inside my chest
and my stomach churns.

The Concert Is Two Weeks Away

At dinner,
I tell my family,

"The concert is two weeks away.
Please come."
Aria groans,
but Maman gives her a look.
"Of *course* we'll be there,"
Maman says.

"You've been working
so hard," Daddy says.

"I wish...," I start to say.
But then I bite off my words
and swallow them.
I almost said,
I wish Strum
would come home for it.

Only Aria notices.
She gives me a long look.
Says, "*I'll* be there,
Maddie."

It's the first time in years that she's called me Maddie.
I almost don't recognize the warmth spreading through
me.

Part of You

Later, when we're getting ready
for bed,

I tell Aria,
"I'm too nervous.
Whenever I think about
the concert,
I feel sick."

"You'll be fine,"
she says.
"You've played that solo
so many times,
it's become
part of you. Part of all of us.
I could play that solo."

"Aria!"

She dances out of my reach,
laughing.
And despite my fury,
I grin.

Secret Signal

International
Polar Bear Day
is coming soon,
right after the concert.
We make posters in Eco Club
to let everyone know
that disappearing Arctic sea ice

threatens the survival
of polar bears.
And humans, really.

Ms. Vidal gives Emma and me
permission to put up the posters.
As we tape them
in the hallway—
Emma taping,
me making sure they're
absolutely straight—
she sighs.
"Wish I could sit next to Oliver
in orchestra.
He's so hot."

I laugh.
"Emma! Ewww. He's definitely
not hot."

She giggles.
"Oh, I bet I know who you like,"
she says. "Danny."
A nervous giggle bubbles up
inside me.
"But Topher likes you," she adds
with a wicked grin. "I can tell."

"Topher! Ack! No way."

Emma shushes me
before we get in trouble.

We choke back our giggles.
I don't even want to think about
Topher. It makes
my neck hot.

"This one is crooked," I say,
removing the poster and
          repositioning it,
even though Emma
gives me a funny look.
But everything
needs to be
perfect.

To distract her I say,
"Emma, I'm nervous
about my solo.
Every time we rehearse,
my stomach wobbles."

"Let's try a secret signal," she says.
"I'll blink at you from the clarinet section.
Three times.
That means, '*You got this.*'"
She blinks with each word.
"Would that help?"

Three is not a good number
but I thank her anyway.

It is only on the bus home after school
that I remember

Emma doesn't have a solo.
Two eighth-grade clarinetists
have them all.
And she never said a word.

I shouldn't have talked about my solo.

No Unclaimed Bodies

Detective Sanderson
visits to bring us up to date.
When Maman told him
my new theory,
the detectives searched the database
for public cameras
near the southern border.

"At first," he says,
"we didn't think we'd find
anything. As you know,
we'd already checked out
all the anonymous tips
and the morgues
in all
the surrounding states.
No unclaimed bodies fit
your son's description."

I suck in my breath
at the same time as Aria.

Why did he have to mention
bodies?
Maman's face looks waxy.
Daddy's jaw tightens.
I swallow against the heaviness
in the pit of my stomach.
Count the hairs
that flop over Gizmo's eyes
as he dozes near my feet.
Making sure they
come out even.

Aria Reaches Out

Aria reaches out. Squeezes my hand tight.
I squeeze back and it makes me feel light.

A Grainy Photo

Detective Sanderson
keeps talking.
"Then we found this."

He shows us a grainy photo
on his phone.
"This was taken
in a bus station in
El Paso, Texas,

four weeks
after your son disappeared."

We lean in to look.
It could be Strum.
He's wearing
a different jacket.
The figure in the grainy photo
looks thin
and older,
with a scraggly beard,
like a homeless person.

Then I realize
Strum *is*
a homeless person.
Four weeks on the road,
eating very little,
sleeping in the open,
would change someone.

"C'est lui," Maman says.
"That's definitely him."

I count to myself,
mid-November to
mid-February.
That is how long
Strum has been
gone now.
Three months.
Not a good number.

Has he really been heading for the
Mexican rainforest
all this time?

That night
Maman and Daddy
start planning a trip
to Mexico City.

The Whole Is Equal to the Sum of Its Parts

In geometry, Nico taps my arm
with his pencil.
"What's wrong?"
he asks in a loud whisper.
"I mean, besides the usual."

Mrs. Turner looks over at us,
arches one eyebrow.
"Quiet, please!"
We're supposed to be
doing classwork.

"What's wrong?"
Nico asks again.
I shake my head.
"Later," I whisper.

There's too much
going on.

Strum.
The solo.
Maman and Daddy
leaving for Mexico
tomorrow.
It'll be back to
Aria and me
and scary sounds in the night.

I count the equals signs
in the worksheet.
Onetwothreefourfivesixseven.
Not a good number.

I concentrate on the next problem
and remind myself
the whole is equal
to the sum of its parts.
$AB + BC = AC$
Geometry usually
calms me down.
But my knees shake,
my fingers twitch.

After class,
Nico walks me to the main doors.
"So, are you going to tell me
what's wrong?"

I tell him
that my parents are flying
to Mexico to look for Strum.

I tell him
I'll be stuck here with Aria
again.

I tell him
my concert is
five days away
and I feel like I'm going to be sick
when I think about the solo.
"And I don't know if my parents
will be back by then."

He nods.
"I'll come to your concert
with Aria. So even if your parents
aren't back yet,
you'll have some fans."
He grins.
I try to smile back.

"And believe it or not,"
he adds,
"I used to practically throw up
before a concert."

"Is that why you stopped playing?"
I ask.
"Naw," he says. "I got interested
in other things. Movies, plays.
I even write poetry,
but don't tell my friends that."

"I won't," I say, smiling. "I don't know
your friends."
His laughter is a burst of sun
after a storm.

"So how did you keep
from throwing up
when you were nervous?"

He taps his forehead.
"Mind power.
In your head,
go to a place where you felt calm."
He grins.
"You can do this, muchachita."

The Night Before

The night before
the concert,
I talk to
Maman and Daddy
on the phone.
"We're so sorry we
won't be there,"
Daddy says.

"But we're getting close,"
Maman says.

"We just arrived in Tuxtla Gutiérrez,
the capital of Chiapas."

"Chiapas?" I ask.

"It's a state in Mexico," Maman says.
"There's a beautiful cathedral here.
We've shown Strum's photo
to dozens of people in the squares
and two people
recognized him.
One woman said
she'd seen him
yesterday,
at an open-air market."

Maman takes a deep breath.
"Je suis certaine."
I am certain.
"We will
find him
soon."

Something surges
inside me
like the finale
of *Bolero*
and threatens to
burst out
as joy.

Dear Family

I'm getting dressed for the concert.
Black pants and a white button-up shirt.
Everyone will look like Oliver tonight.

Aria shouts outside my door. "Woo-hoo!"
She knocks. "Can I come in?"

I say, "Sure," and finish tucking in my shirt.

Her face glows. "Did you see? Did you see?
The email?"

"What email?" I shake my head.
"I was getting dressed."

"From Strum!"

"What?" I sit down hard
on the side of my bed.
Strum? Strum's alive?
"You got an email from Strum?!"

"You did too, silly. He wrote to all of us!"
All of us? I think. *Even Daddy?*
"Well, you and Maman and me."

Aria sits next to me,
reads the email aloud.

"Dear Family,

I'm so sorry I walked away
without a word. Sorry I put you
through that.

I was in a dark place
and it took me a long time
to sort through everything.

By the time I arrived in Mexico City,
I finally realized I needed help,
so I checked into a clinic
for a few weeks.
They straightened me out
enough to know what I need to do.

From there, I made my way
to Tuxtla Gutiérrez,
where I'm living now.
It's a beautiful city.
I'm working in a market
temporarily
but I'd like to stay
in Tuxtla.
I've decided to write to the dean
of my university, apologize,
ask to take a year off.
I'm hoping to find a job here
building affordable housing."

I sigh. That's Strum.
Thinking of those in need.

But not of us.
Aria shakes her head, bites her lip.

"Wait! He said he's in Tuxtla.
That's where Maman and Daddy are now!"
I brush the hair out of my face.
"Do you think they'll find him?"

Aria nods. "I do."

I glance at her, shivering.
Aria is the last person I thought
would still have faith.

She looks at her phone. "Wow!
Look what time it is!
We have to go now or you'll be late
for your concert."

Concert?
Deep breath. Another.
"Maybe I should just
forget the concert."

She grabs my hands and pulls me up.
"Oh, no, Maddie. You've worked
too hard for this. Let's go!
Nico's meeting us there."

She heads for the door.
"And bring your phone.
You can call Maman
while I'm driving."

Over the Moon

In the car,
before I get a chance
to call Maman,
my phone rings.

"Maddie! Je suis aux anges!"
I am over the moon.
Maman's voice dances like a butterfly.
"Did you read the email?"

"Yes, yes! Isn't it
fantastic?" I can't stop grinning.

"And he's *here*! In Tuxtla!"

Daddy's voice breaks in.
"We'll find him tomorrow,
and if he still wants to go,
we'll take him to that nature preserve."

"Montes Azules Biosphere Reserve," I say.
"And Laguna Miramar."
I smile at Aria, who gives me a quick grin,
then turns her eyes back to the road.

"That's the place," Daddy says.
"It's about a hundred and forty miles from here.
But we'll get him there
if he wants to go."

It's been years since
Daddy wanted to be kind to Strum.

Daddy's voice falters.
"After that…"

I know what he's trying to say.
After that, Strum won't be coming home.
At least, not yet.

But I miss him. I want him home.

The Meaning of Three

As we tune our instruments
in the gym, which is also
the auditorium,
I can't stop thinking about Strum.
Wishing I could have talked to him.
Wishing he would come home.

My stomach won't stop
bubbling like a volcano.
I don't want to be sick.
What was it Nico said to do?
Oh, right.
*In your head, go to a place
where you felt calm.*

Ignoring the organized chaos
of forty-four instruments
tuning up,
I close my eyes and go
to the Butterfly Farm.

Count slowly,
one
two
three
four
deep breaths, in and out.
Sun filters through
banana leaves.
Blue morphos flutter,
appearing and
disappearing.
Strum and I laugh,
chasing them.

The rapid tempo of my pulse
slows down.

Strum said,
Music is your superpower.

Aria said,
It's become part of you.

Nico said,
You can do this.

I open my eyes to see
Aria and Nico
waving and smiling
from the bleachers.
I smile back.

Two sections over,
Danny and Bethann wave at me
while Topher makes goofy faces.
I laugh.

So many people cheering me on.
Music lets us
speak the same language.

Next to me, Oliver gives
a thumbs-up.
I give him
a thumbs-up back.
He has solos too.

Then Emma blinks three times
at me
from the clarinet section.
Our secret signal.
You got this.

Maybe three is not always
a bad number. Not when it means
you got this.
Not when it really means
friend.

Maybe tomorrow I will
sign Emma up for
a polar bear adoption.
And pay for it with the money
I didn't spend on that bus ride.

If anyone should adopt
a polar bear,
it's Emma.

The Concert

Mr. Dahlberg
raises his baton.
It's time.

A slight pause. And
the concert begins.

Mouthing my reed,
I think of ducks, polar bears,
and butterflies.

Bright blue morphos appear and disappear.

When I play my solo, music starts
deep within me,
expanding, rising, until
it surges outward, like a butterfly
emerging from its chrysalis.

I play for Strum,
hoping he will escape from the wolf
of what's troubling him.

I play for my family.

I play for my friends.

I play for anyone
who is lost.

The music fills me. The music
is me.
It's my heartbeat,
pulsing bright blue.

As I finish the last measures, I picture us five,
     Strum and Aria, Maman, Daddy, and me,
walking through southeastern Mexico.

Apart or together,
we will always be a family.

I hope Daddy will try harder
to understand Strum.
I hope Strum
will forgive Daddy's
stubbornness.

My last drawn-out notes are an anguished cry:
Please
let us learn to get along.

I imagine the harmony of being together.
Heading out to the lake called Laguna Miramar.

As we near the lake, we see
glimpses of blue, then bright flashes
of blue, and now
there is
blueblueblueblue
everywhere.

Blue morphos flying free!

ACKNOWLEDGMENTS

This book has been a long time coming and I have many people to thank. My deepest apologies if I missed someone.

My parents, who raised me with books, music, and love. Only recently have I realized just how fortunate this made me.

My editor, Sally Morgridge, and her team at Holiday House, for helping me make this novel the best it can possibly be. Thanks especially to Eryn Levine, Elizabeth Law, Mary Cash, Raina Putter, Terry Borzumato-Greenberg, Michelle Montague, Emily Mannon, Sara DiSalvo, Kerry Martin, and Elena Megalos. It's been a joy working with you.

My agent, Barbara Krasner, for believing in this book right from the start.

SCBWI, which I joined in December 2007, for workshops and inspiration, but especially for the friendships I formed with so many writers I can't possibly name you all. I appreciate each one of you.

The Highlights Foundation, for the magic and the fabulous food. I was fortunate enough to attend two workshops on Novels in Verse, mentored by Kathryn Erskine and Alma Fullerton, with special guest Padma Venkatraman. Thank you all.

My fellow Highlights attendees, for the valuable feedback and encouragement. From the 2016 group: Jan Godown Annino, Leah Rosti (also one of my beta readers), Ray Anthony Shepard, Linda Mitchell, Leah Henderson, Elena Radulescu, Marcie Flinchum Atkins, and Danielle Joseph.

From the 2017 Highlights group: Dede Fox, Kip Wilson, Charles Waters, Traci Sorell, Susan Santiago, and Caroline Montgelas.

My beta readers, who provided excellent feedback: Tara Videon, Jeannine Quain Norris, Christine Danek, Dianne Salerni, Jennifer Lovin Williams, Myrna Foster, Lauren Leibman, and Barbara Goren.

A huge thank you to Caroline Starr Rose for her insightful critique.

Special thanks to reader Ilene Wong (author I. W. Gregorio), for her help with Emma and her mother (and those dumplings!), and to my college friend Jennifer Humbert, for the foreign language help. Any remaining errors are my own.

My niece, Susan Gregory, a high school teacher, for filling me in on school schedules.

Author friends, for inspiration, advice, and encouragement, including Nicole Valentine, Amy Garvey, K. M. Walton, A. S. King, Beth Kephart, Laurie Halse Anderson, Ellen Jensen Abbott, Jessica Lawson, Katia Raina, Joanne Ryder, Laurence Yep, and Jerry and Eileen Spinelli.

My family, who had so much to deal with the last few years because of my devastating illness. Eric and Kurt, I love you more than words can say. Thank you for everything.

Last, but never least, my husband, Carl, who has been by my side for more than thirty-five years. I couldn't have done this without you.